This book belongs to:

.....Rebecca...........

.....Fraser...............

MY BOOK OF

animal

STORIES

MY BOOK OF

animal

STORIES

Written by
NICOLA BAXTER

Illustrated by
SASCHA LIPSCOMB

This is a Parragon Book
First published in 2000

Parragon
Queen Street House
4 Queen Street
Bath BA1 1HE, UK

ISBN 0-75253-511-0

Produced for Parragon by
Nicola Baxter
PO Box 215
Framingham Earl
Norwich NR14 7UR

Designed by Amanda Hawkes

Printed in Italy

Contents

The Real Dog   9

Batty Cat's Nineteen Lives   31

The Particular Parrot   55

Mr. Ribble and the Rabbit   77

The Ambitious Hippo   103

Lucy Had a Little Goat   125

The Impossible Pony   149

Wilfred, the Wanderer   173

The Lazy Leopards   199

The Perfect Polar Bear   221

Tortoise Trouble   245

Dinosaur Doom   267

The Real Dog

When Thomas first said he would like a dog, his father said, "No! There will be no discussion about it, Tom. You are not having a dog and that's final."

The next time Thomas mentioned how wonderful it would be to have a dog of his very own, his father said, "No! I don't want to talk about it any more. We'll think about it when you are older."

The third time that Thomas raised the subject of a dog in the house, his father said, "No! One day you will be able to have one, I expect. But at the moment I know who would end up cleaning up after it and feeding it." (He didn't mean himself. He meant Thomas's mother.)

When Thomas suggested for the fourth time that a dog would be a really wonderful addition to his life, his father said, "No! No, no, no, no, NO! Well, all right then."

But that didn't mean that Thomas's difficulties were over.

"It's very important what kind of dog you choose, Tom," said his father. "I know a thing or two about dogs, and I can tell you that what you need is a *proper* dog. Not one of those little ratty things with short legs. You want something like a labrador, or a dalmation, or a setter."

Thomas's mother sighed.

"A labrador, or a dalmation, or a setter will need to run for miles and miles each day," she said. "You won't have time to do it and go to school, Tom. I know perfectly well who will end up roaming the countryside with your pet."

"You'd enjoy the exercise," said her husband. "I simply won't have a dog in the house that reminds me of a hairbrush, no matter how cute he is."

"But…" said Tom.

"But…" said Tom's mother.

"That's my final word," said Tom's father. "And I have nothing more to say on the subject."

As it turned out, Tom's father had quite a lot more nothing to say on the subject. On Monday, he said there was no way he would ever be seen with anything smaller than a sheepdog. On Tuesday, he said that his mind was made up that the legs of a spaniel were the shortest he would consider. On Wednesday, he spoke quite favourably about corgis, which he said were owned by some very important people, so the shortness of their legs didn't count. On Thursday, he warmed to the subject of terriers and remembered fondly a little white dog owned by his favourite uncle twenty years before.

On Friday, when Tom's father was explaining to anyone who would listen that some small dogs had a great deal of spirit, Tom's mother suggested that they all go down to the Rescue Centre to see what kind of dogs were available.

"Yes, then I ... I mean we ... I mean Tom ... will be able to make a sensible choice," said Tom's father.

It was exciting being at the Rescue Centre. Thomas couldn't wait to start looking at the dogs, but first a lady with a clipboard asked them to sit down while she took some details and found out if they could offer a dog the kind of home it needed. The first part, when she asked for names and addresses was fine. When she got to the bit about what kind of dog they were looking for, things became a good deal trickier. Naturally, it was Tom's father who caused the trouble.

"We are looking," he said firmly, "that is, Tom is looking for a dog with long legs ... but not too long."

The lady's pen hovered over her clipboard.

"Which would mean...?" she asked, with a puzzled expression.

"Medium legs," said Tom's father.

"I was hoping," said the lady, with a noticeably colder tone, "that you would describe the *temperament* you would prefer in a dog."

"Lively," said Tom's father.

"Quiet," said Tom's mother.

"Friendly," said Tom.

"You have discussed this, have you, as a family?" asked the lady.

"Definitely," said Tom's father.

"Sort of," said Tom's mother.

"No one asked me," said Tom.

The lady put away her clipboard.

"I think you should all come back when you have sorted out what you really want," she said.

Tom was almost in tears. He could hear exciting sounds of barking behind the swing doors. It was horrible to be so near and yet so far from his dream. His mother, seeing his face, saved the day.

"I hope that's not necessary," she said. "What we need is a nice, friendly dog that my son could look after by himself— with our supervision, of course. A small dog would be best, but one with plenty of character. We will do everything we can to give him a happy life with us."

The lady softened.

"Perhaps you had better go and see the dogs we have at the moment," she said. "We can meet back here in fifteen minutes. I can then tell you more about any dog you are particularly interested in."

They saw lively dogs with tails that wagged non-stop.

They saw shy, retiring dogs that needed to be cuddled.

They saw tiny dogs.

They saw huge dogs.

And they saw Rags.

"There he is!" cried Tom, as if he had know Rags all his life. "It's him! Look!" Dad, *please* don't say anything to upset that lady!"

Thomas's father was about to protest, but Rags put his head on one side so comically that he had to laugh instead.

"He's a very fine dog," he said. "And I can see that he's exactly right for you, Tom. Even if his legs still have some growing to do."

Luckily, the lady agreed that Rags *was* exactly right for Tom. She arranged to come around to inspect Tom's house the next morning. Then, if everything was in order, Tom could take Rags home.

All the way home, Tom's mother and father talked about the tidying and sorting they would have to do to make sure the lady was happy the next day. But Tom just sat in the back of the car with a big smile on his face.

"I know it will be all right," he said. "Rags was waiting for me. I could see that straight away."

Thomas was right. The lady was happy to see that the family had a big garden with a tall fence. She was pleased that Tom's mother had thought about where the little dog would sleep and Tom's father had put anything that could be chewed high up out of reach. That very same afternoon, the family went to collect Rags and take him to his new home.

It was as if the little dog had always been there. Within a week, none of the family could remember what it had been like to come home and not see a cheeky little face peering through the window. They asked themselves how they had ever managed to enjoy country walks without a naughty little dog to dive into ditches and chase squirrels.

As for Tom, he and Rags were the closest of friends. Tom told Rags all his troubles and all his dreams. And Rags

would put his head on one side and seem
to understand everything.

"It's really sweet to see them,"
Tom's mother told his father, as they
watched their son playing with Rags in the
garden one day.

"I know," said her husband. "I'm
glad to feel that I made the right choice."

For a whole year, Rags was part of
the family. Then, one awful August day,
something dreadful happened. A huge
truck, rattling too fast around a corner
near Tom's home, lost control and

smashed through the fence into the back garden. There was terrible damage to the fence, the flowerbeds and the garage, but none of that mattered to the family. Rags had been sleeping under a bench. Now he would sleep for ever.

Without Rags, the house seemed cold and empty. Everyone had the feeling that they would walk into a room and see his cheerful little face once more. But they didn't. Rags had gone.

After a few months, Tom's mother and father talked about what they should do. Tom was very quiet and pale these days. They were worried about him.

"I think we should get another dog," said Tom's father. "It's like falling off a horse. You have to get straight back on again. And besides, looking after a new dog would take Tom's mind off it. He really hasn't accepted that Rags has gone."

For once, Tom's father was right. When the little boy's parents gently told him of their plan, he looked shocked.

"Oh no," he said, "I don't think that Rags would like that at all."

"What do you mean, darling?" asked Tom's mother.

"There's only room for one dog in this house," said Tom firmly, "and that's Rags. I don't need another dog while I've got him."

Tom's mother and father tried to explain that Rags was not coming back. But the more they tried, the more Tom insisted that they were wrong. He started taking Rags for walks again. At least, he took Rags' lead for walks. Each morning he put out fresh water and biscuits. Each evening, he said goodnight to Rags and patted an imaginary head before he went upstairs for his bath before bed.

"I don't know what to do," Tom's mother told her husband. "It's just so sad. Do you think we should take him to see someone? I can't bear to think of him having to pretend like this."

"Let's give it a few more weeks," replied Tom's father. "One day he'll just forget to pretend, and then Rags really will be gone."

But Tom wasn't really pretending. There was a Rags-shaped place in his heart

that simply had to be filled. Life without
Rags was impossible to imagine. Only he
did miss being able to cuddle the warm,
wriggly little dog. He missed the feel of
Rags' rough little tongue on his cheek. He
even missed being told off about dirty
pawmarks on the knees of his trousers.
But he wouldn't let himself miss Rags.
Rags hadn't really gone. He knew that.

   "I think you were right after
all about getting another dog,"
said Tom's father to his
wife one evening.
"We can't go on
like this, and I
miss having a
dog around the
place. Tom will
get used to the
idea, although it may take some time for
him to become fond of another one."

But Tom's parents didn't have to go out and find another dog. Another dog found them.

One night shortly before Christmas, Tom was watching a TV programme when he suddenly looked up.

"I can hear something outside," he said. "I'm going to look."

"It's dark, Tom," protested his mother, walking behind him down the hall. "You can't go outside in this weather."

But Tom was already opening the front door. He peered out into the snow, but there was nothing to be seen.

"I thought I heard Rags," he said softly, hanging his head.

Tom's mother knew that the moment had come to talk about it all.

"I thought you felt Rags was still in here with us," she said gently, closing the door. "He can't be out there, too."

"It isn't the real Rags here with us," confessed Tom, starting to cry. "He's never quite here. And sometimes now, I can't see him at all. You know, the first time I ever saw him, it was like I'd been missing him for years already. It's like that again now. I keep waiting for him to turn up again."

Tom's mother gave him a big hug and let him cry.

"I think you have to let Rags go, sweetheart," she said. "He had a happy time with us, but that happy time is past. Don't you think it might be time to be happy with another dog? It wouldn't be Rags, of course, but I'm sure we would all grow to love it just as we did with that naughty little dog."

"I don't know," whispered Tom. "It would have to be Rags again, you see. I mean, it would have to be a little dog that I sort of knew before I ever saw him. And I don't think that could happen again. I've been hoping that Rags has been waiting somewhere, waiting to come back to us."

"Let's go back and sit down," said his mother. "I'll make you a drink."

But just then, there was a little scrabbling sound from outside. Tom's mother saw the hope flare up in her son's eyes, and her heart went out to the little boy as he ran to the door.

There on the doorstep sat a little dog. It wasn't Rags. It didn't look at all like Rags. But somehow… Tom frowned.

"I'm not imagining it," he said. "I'm not. I'm not."

Then, all of a sudden, the visitor put his head on one side in a way that was so, so familiar.

The little dog trotted in through the front door and wiped his feet carefully on the doormat. Thomas knew then that he *must* be imagining it. Dogs *never* wipe their feet. But the little dog walked straight into the living room and settled down in front of the television. He turned to look at Thomas, as if saying, "Come on, I'm waiting for you."

Thomas sat down beside the little dog. Very slowly he reached out his hand. Under his fingers he felt a warm, soft, living, breathing body.

"Welcome back, Rags," he said.

Batty Cat's Nineteen Lives

People sometimes ask me why our cat is called Batty Cat. That just goes to show that they don't know our family very well and they don't know Batty Cat at all. You only have to spend ten minutes in the company of our cat to discover that he is well and truly batty. What other cat would try to catch the goldfish in the pond by swimming after them? What other cat would try to walk along the linen line? What other cat likes to eat old socks?

Batty Cat is a cat of mystery. No one knows where he came from. He simply turned up in our kitchen one day and never went away. Sometimes I wonder if somewhere there is a snorkeling, tight-rope-walking sock-eating pensioner just waiting for Batty Cat to come home, but the thought is too horrible. On the other hand, it's hard to imagine Batty Cat with a family any saner than ours.

But then, if I'm being truthful, our family isn't very sane. Mum painted the house purple last week. Dad has a massive collection of old phone books. Mags, my little sister, is totally bonkers—the way that only little sisters can be. Batty Cat, as you can see, fits right in.

When Batty Cat arrived, it was pretty obvious that he had already lived quite a life. His nose was scarred, he had a chunk missing from one ear, and there was a kink in his tail that suggested he had once caught it in a car door or something. We didn't think much about this until he lost his first life with us. You know how cats are supposed to have nine lives, losing one each time they have a narrow escape? Well, Batty had a narrow escape about half an hour after he arrived in our kitchen.

It was a Saturday morning. Mags was keen on acrobatics at the time and was hanging upside down from the kitchen door frame. Mum was having one of her enthusiasms for healthiness and was busy cooking something brown and solid on the stove. During these times, everything we ate was brown and solid. Mum had to tell us whether she was offering us beef

stew, chocolate cake or nut roast. It didn't make any difference. They all tasted like cardboard.

At the table, Dad was trying to build one of his matchstick models. That's his other hobby—phone books and matchstick models keep him occupied all the time that he's at home. He doesn't even watch telly, which is embarrassing when you're with friends and he asks, "What's a Klingon?"

I was cleaning my football boots. I sometimes think I'm the only normal person here. I play football. I watch football. I read football magazines and eat football-shaped cereal. And you needn't even think about offering me a drink if it's not in my red and white mug.

Anyway, I was cleaning my boots at the sink and quite a bit of mud was flying into Mum's cooking, but when something is brown and solid already, a bit of mud doesn't make a lot of difference.

As far as I remember (it all got a bit confused for a while), Mum bent down and took a large tin of something the colour of liver and the consistency of concrete out of the oven. She was carrying it across the kitchen, and I swear I was only practising a free kick with the shoe-cleaner can, when she suddenly crashed to

the floor. The tin of gunk flew up into the air, smashed the light bulb and hurtled down again. None of us noticed to start with that it landed with a sort of *thunk* instead of a crash on the tiled floor, as we were all looking at Mum.

Our mother isn't the most graceful woman in the world. She's constantly falling over something or off something or into something. So we didn't really think she had hurt herself, but it's only right to look up when your mother hits the deck. In fact, she was on her hands and knees, peering under the fridge and saying, "It must be three years since I cleaned under there, but I don't feel like doing it now."

We all went back to doing what we were doing, until Mags, coming down from a sort of somersault, suddenly cried out, "Oh, Mum, you've killed the cat!"

"We haven't got a cat," said Dad. But we had. Somewhere in the confusion, Batty had entered our lives and was now lying very still on the kitchen floor with a tin of something brown and solid on his head. He certainly didn't look lively.

Mags and Mum crouched over the body while Dad and I stood about feeling awkward. You can't just carry on when there's a dead cat in the middle of your kitchen, but on the other hand, we didn't see what we could do about it.  Dad shut the back door, perhaps thinking we could only deal with one dead cat at a time and it would be best to avoid any more of them turning up their toes in our old kitchen.

Very gently, Mum lifted the tin off the cat's head, and the cat gave a little groan and a sigh.

"It's alive!" cried Mum and Mags together, as if they were in a hospital drama on telly. The cat moaned and sighed again, and I don't know what it was, but maybe the thought of telly programmes put it into my head. I suddenly felt that the moan and the sigh were fake. That cat was acting! When he did the moan and sigh a third time, and put one paw over his forehead, I was certain. I went over and peered down at him. Slowly, he opened one yellow eye. I'm quite sure he winked.

Anyway, Mum and Mags spent the rest of the day running around after the cat, taking him to the vet, feeding him milk and sardines, and generally making a fuss of him.

"You can't practise football in the hall," they said, "you might hurt the cat."

"You can't watch the match," they said, "the cat needs peace and quiet."

"You can't have your supper yet," they said, "we're still looking after the poor little cat."

It's amazing that I didn't start hating that cat there and then, but even at the beginning I had a grudging admiration for him. I mean, he was milking it (if you'll excuse the term) for all he was worth. Mum and Mags decided to call him Patrick, because it happened to be Saint Patrick's Day. That was before we all knew quite how batty he was.

Later that evening, Pat the cat was well enough to wander around and get his bearings. At first Mum and Mags followed him everywhere, to make sure he was all right. After a while, since he was doing normal cat-like things, such as sitting on the beds and digging his claws into the sofas, they left him to it. Mum made suppr at last and for once it wasn't brown and solid. As we were running so late, she opened some tins and we had something orange and squelchy instead. Then, after some prompting from me, she threw my football kit into the washing machine for the match the next day and rushed off to take Mags to her gymnastics class.

I don't know what made me go into the dark little passageway where the washing machine is kept. I think I was looking for an old pair of boots. As I passed, I happened to glance at the machine, which was just starting to fill and spin. A furry little face was pressed to the glass.

Well, I stopped the machine and opened the door as quickly as I could, flooding the passageway with water and ruining my old boots for ever. The cat came out in a rush with the water and half skidded under the boiler.

This time, I thought he was dead for sure. When I picked him up, he was limp and wet. He looked half his normal size with wet fur. I once saw a programme where a farmer tried to revive a newborn kitten by rubbing it in a rough towel, and that was all I could think to do. I picked up the cat and hurtled up the stairs with it and into the bathroom. ThenI rubbed it as hard as I could and tried holding it upside down to get the water out. I've since been told I did all the wrong things, so please don't try it at home, but by sheer luck Pat the cat started moving. In a minute or two, he sat up in the towel and shook himself.

He looked absolutely fine. I carried him downstairs and laid him, still wrapped in the towel, on the sofa to recover. Then it was my turn to do the milk-and-sardines routine. Only…

While I was in the kitchen, Dad came into the living room and sat down to look at one of his telephone directories.

When I came back into the room, carrying Pat the cat's snack, there was no sign of him.

"Where's the cat?" I asked.

"He wasn't here when I came in," said Dad. I knew I had shut the door. A horrible suspicion began to grow in my mind as I looked at my father.

"Dad," I said, trying not to panic, "just get up for a moment, would you?"

Dad could see I was serious and heaved himself to his feet. There on the sofa was the towel. In the middle of the towel were two little ears. But the towel didn't move.

This time, I thought the cat must really be dead for sure. My dad's not a small man, and our sofa isn't particularly squashy. But a second later, the cat lifted its head and gave a little yowl.

Dad and I spent the rest of the evening taking the cat to the vet (again). The vet looked at us strangely, as if we were the kind of people who made a habit

of concussing, drowning and squashing cats, but in the end he said there was nothing really wrong and let us take him home. Pat the cat stretched out in the box we brought him in and settled down to sleep.

That evening, when Mum and Mags were back from gymnastics, we called a special family meeting to talk about what to do with the cat. Most of us had done him some damage at some time during the day, so we felt responsible for him. It was decided that we would put up notices in the local shop, and if no one claimed him, we would keep him. It was sometime during the meeting that Mags started to call him Patty Cat, and the rest of us called out at once, "No, let's call him Batty Cat!" The name stuck.

It was also during that meeting that Mags brought up the subject of a cat's nine lives and how many Batty had left.

"He used up three this afternoon," she said. "That means he only has six left."

"From the looks of him, he's used up quite a few already," said Dad. "His scarred nose, his kinky tail and the chunk out of his ear must account for another three lives at least."

"The vet said he'd already had quite a few bumps and bashes," said Mum. "I doubt if he's got any lives left at all."

But Mags couldn't bear that. She claimed that he was a special cat, with not nine but nineteen lives, and she looked so eager that we agreed with her. By the end of his first day with us, we reckoned, Batty was on his tenth life and counting.

Over the next few weeks, Batty Cat seemed to have suicidal tendencies. He tried climbing the chimney from the inside just before Mum lit the fire. He tried sleeping in the oven just before Mum cooked the supper. He even tried sharpening his claws on one of Dad's matchstick models, which caused Dad to hurl a phone book at him from across the room. It wasn't a good plan. The book missed the cat and smashed the model, damaging the section on Architectural Ironmongery at the same time. Batty fled.

As the weeks passed, Batty's quota of lives was getting used up pretty quickly. When he got his head stuck in the milk jug and almost drowned, he reached number nineteen. We all felt a sense of dread. Next time might be *it* for Batty Cat.

By now, of course, we couldn't imagine life without that animal. He did the most extraordinary things—diving into a trifle when Aunt Muriel came to lunch, eating Mum's most solid and brown inventions with enthusiasm, lying on the bonnet of the car with all four feet in the air—but we all felt that he was a most extraordinary cat. And we wouldn't know what to do without him.

At last Mags said what we were all thinking.

"It's like having something really horrible hanging over you," she said. "It's as if we're just waiting for something awful to happen. Why don't we keep an eye on him instead? So that it can't."

After that, we tried hard to keep a round-the-clock watch on Batty Cat. It proved to be impossible. How do you follow a cat who is walking along telephone wires? Who can stay awake while he prowls around the neighbourhood visiting his lady friends, especially the little tabby cat next door? After a week, we gave up.

Then something really wonderful happened. Batty Cat got run over by a car. It may not sound wonderful to you, and of course it wasn't much fun for Batty Cat, who gained another kink in his tail and a very sore leg, but we were delighted. Batty had used up not nineteen but twenty lives, and he was still with us. We didn't have to worry after all. Some cats obviously have hundreds of lives, and Batty was one of them.

Batty is quite an old cat now, although he still does daft things. He tried hang-gliding from Mags' kite. He tried highboard-diving into the watering can. He stole some snacks from the Doberman down the street and ate them in full view. He still eats Mum's cooking, although brown and solid things have now become greenish-yellow squelchy things, as she's become obsessed by vegetables.

Still, we all know that Batty won't be with us for ever, and until this morning we dreaded the day.

This morning, however, Batty came into the kitchen with something dangling from his mouth.

"Ugh! It's a rat!" cried Mags.

"Is it dead?" asked Dad, thinking of little teeth gnawing his matchsticks.

But it wasn't a rat. It was a kitten, a little striped kitten who looked exactly like Batty Cat. And it immediately tried to climb up the table leg and fell into Batty's sardines.

There is no doubt about it. Batty the Second has come to stay, and we couldn't be happier.

The Particular Parrot

My Aunt Margaret is one of those people who is always helping others. When her next-door neighbour has a cold, Aunt Margaret is there with bowls of soup and advice about woollen underwear. When the local primary school asks for knitted teddy bears to sell on behalf of orphans on the other side of the world, my Aunt Margaret knits furiously for weeks. You can't sit down in her living room without squashing half a dozen bears in various stages of completion.

In one way, it's very good that she throws herself whole-heartedly into whatever she is doing. In another way, it can be a bit scary. I mean, would you think it was possible that someone could knit six hundred teddy bears in a month? When does she find time to eat?

Helpful as she is to anyone who asks, Aunt Margaret saves most of her energy for the oldest of her neighbours. If you're ninety, beware! Aunt Margaret will bring you food, do your washing, take your letters to the post and tidy your room—whether you want her to or not! I once witnessed a pitiful tug-of-war as an old lady tried to hold on to her oldest and most comfortable slippers.

"They're past it," Aunt Margaret said firmly. "They're a health hazard. Look at these nice new slippers I've brought you."

The old lady kept a fierce grip on her slippers with her gnarled fingers.

"They're my favourite slippers and I want to keep them," she said.

Aunt Margaret tugged in her turn. "What for?" she asked. "You can't wear them with holes like this in the soles. You'll fall over."

"I just want to *look* at them," said the old lady. "That's not dangerous, surely?"

Of course, it was an unequal contest. Aunt Margaret gained possession of the slippers and would not let go.

"I'll make us a nice hot drink," she said. "It will be soothing."

When she had bustled into the kitchen, the old lady turned to me.

"I don't want you to think I'm losing my marbles," she sighed. "Of course I don't want those wretched old slippers. I was about to throw them out anyway. It's just the priniciple of the thing. Your aunt is a lovely woman, but she does like to have her own way. And so do I!"

I quite often went with my aunt to see the senior citizens. I liked them. They had lots of interesting things to talk about and they very often had tins of toffees hidden somewhere. Also, they liked to have their rooms really warm, and I live with my brothers and sisters in a huge, draughty old house. I liked their snug rooms. I even liked the way they usually had the telly on. It's amazing what you can learn on daytime television.

There's only one big problem about getting fond of really old people, and that is that sometimes they leave quite suddenly, before you've had a chance to say goodbye. I don't mean that they die, although that does happen, of course. I mean that they go to live with sons and daughters, or move into homes. That's what happened to Harry Baggle.

Harry Baggle was a jolly old man with a white beard around his chin and no hair at all on top of his head.

"It slipped," he said, the first time he caught me peering at his face. Somehow, he always made me wonder if he'd put his head on the right way up. Some elderly people like you to call them Mr. or Mrs. or

Miss. Some of them like you to use their first names, which are usually something odd like Gladys or Ethel or Gilbert. Harry Baggle had other ideas.

"Call me Cap'n," he said, the first time I met him. "I've been used to it all my life and I'm not going to be plain Mister now. You can't teach an old sea dog new tricks, you know."

"Aye, aye, Cap'n," I said, which made him laugh.

Unfortunately, it turned out that Cap'n Baggle wasn't a pirate. He used to be in charge of great big oil tankers and cargo ships, taking them all around the world. He had lots of books about huge ships, the bigger the better.

Cap'n Baggle didn't have a proper doorbell. Instead, there was a great big brass bell hanging up outside. You had to give it a big push to make it ring. But that wasn't the most exciting thing about the captain. That was Parrot Perkins.

"I named him after a First Mate of mine," said the captain. "He had the most annoying habit of repeating everything you said to him. Of course, we do that on board ship to make sure an order has been understood. But when I said, 'Pass the mustard, Perkins,' and he replied, 'Passing the mustard, Cap'n,' *every time*, it really got on my nerves. I'm afraid Parrot Perkins here has the same habit, don't you old boy?"

"You old boy," repeated Parrot Perkins, putting his head on one side. He was a big grey parrot and really handsome. He had his own perch in one corner of the room, but most of all he liked to perch on the back of the captain's chair. His huge claws had made rather a mess of the upholstery, which made Aunt Margaret go *tut, tut, tut* every time she came.

Cap'n Baggle and Parrot Perkins were inseparable. When Cap'n Baggle went outdoors, which was less and less as time went on, Parrot Perkins rode on his shoulder. They always drew a crowd when they went into shops, although they were banned from the local supermarket because the parrot ate most of the green-grocery section before they got to the tills.

Unfortunately, it was probably the fact that Parrot Perkins was a big bird that caused the problem. He perched on my shoulder once, and I didn't really like it. Part of me was worried that his great claws would do to my shoulders what he had done to Cap'n Baggle's chair. The other part of me was just overwhelmed by the weight of him. Those parrots are heavier than they look.

Cap'n Baggle, with his tanned, happy face (and his tanned, shiny head) always looked the picture of health. But he was nearly ninety and not as steady on his feet as he used to be.

"You have to balance differently on land," he said to me once, when he almost stumbled in the kitchen. "It's hard to get the hang of when you've been at sea as long as I have."

Of course, Cap'n Baggle had been on shore for nearly thirty years. He should have got his land legs by now, but I didn't think of that at the time.

One fine day, Cap'n Baggle and Parrot Perkins went shopping. The captain bought lots of fruit for his best friend. Maybe it was the weight of his shopping bag, or maybe it was the weight of Parrot Perkins, but when the pair reached the steps by the bus station, they both took a tumble.

Parrot Perkins flapped away with lots of squawks but no scratches. Cap'n Baggle wasn't so lucky. He had broken his leg and broken it badly.

"For a man of his age, that means hospital for several weeks at least," said Aunt Margaret. "We must go to see him and do what we can to help."

I'm quite sure she didn't have in mind the help that Cap'n Baggle asked for.

"You see," he said, sitting up in his hospital bed in red pyjamas and looking remarkably well, "the Animal Rescue place is looking after Parrot Perkins at the moment, and I know he'll hate it. For one thing, that place is full of cats, and if there's one thing Parrot Perkins can't stand, it's cats. He'll be driving them all mad in there. Could you take him home with you, Margaret, just until I'm well enough to come home?"

Aunt Margaret went pale. I knew for sure that she was thinking of her chair-backs and Parrot Perkins' big claws.

"I'm sorry, Harry," she said. (She never would call him Cap'n.) "I really don't think I have the time or the skill to look after a parrot. I wouldn't know where to start. You'll have to ask someone else, I'm afraid."

Cap'n Baggle sighed dramatically.

"They all have cats," he said. Then he put on a truly pitiful expression and sighed again. "I don't know how I can ever get well with Parrot Perkins always on my mind," he said. "I can't sleep. I can't eat. I can't do anything when I'm so worried about my old Perkins."

I thought for a moment that he was going to cry, for he buried his face in the bedclothes and sighed some more. But he lifted one corner of the sheet and gave me an enormous wink.

Aunt Margaret can't resist a person in trouble. She can resist a parrot in trouble quite easily, but Harry Baggle was another matter. The next moment I heard her saying that, of course, she would look after the parrot personally.

"Only," she said with a frown, "how will I know *how* to look after him? I don't know anything about parrots."

"Well, he'll tell you, of course!" grinned the captain. "That *is* a weight off my mind. Would you like a choc?"

Later that afternoon, I went with Aunt Margaret to the Animal Rescue place. They seemed delighted to see us.

"Parrot Perkins? Such a character!" laughed the lady behind the desk, but it sounded a little false to me. I noticed that she backed towards the wall when one of the assistants brought in the parrot. I noticed a nasty look in his eye as well.

Aunt Margaret looked helplessly at the parrot. Just as the captain had promised, the parrot knew just what to do. He hopped on to Aunt Margaret's shoulder and stayed there, flexing his claws in a gentle but slightly menacing manner. I looked at him suspiciously. Now that I'd seen what a good actor the captain was, I was beginning to think that Parrot Perkins might be devious, too.

Back at her house, Aunt Margaret ran around putting old blankets over all the chair-backs. Parrot Perkins watched with something very close to a smile and examined his claws with care, holding up first one foot and then the other. Then he began to whistle.

The whistling gave Aunt Margaret an idea.

"Go and put the kettle on, darling, will you?" she said. "I'm parched, and I wouldn't mind a biscuit, too. It's ages since I had something to eat."

"*Something to eat!*" squawked the parrot, hopping about on a chair.

Aunt Margaret looked at him. Did he mean he was hungry, or was he just copying as he usually did?

"*Pleeeeease!*" said the parrot, which settled the matter.

It was rather fun sitting down to tea with Aunt Margaret and the parrot. Perkins turned out to like plain biscuits much better than the pink wafers that Aunt Margaret usually bought for me. When Aunt Margaret stretched out her hand for the last one, Parrot Perkins made his feelings known.

"*Tut, tut, tut!*" he said, and he sounded so much like Aunt Margaret that I laughed out loud. Even she hurriedly withdrew her hand from the plate and let the parrot lean down and peck up the last biscuit and some crumbs.

It was a few days later when I saw Aunt Margaret again. Usually, she was a plump, cheery-looking person. This was a completely new Aunt Margaret. She looked harrassed. She looked worried. She even looked thinner. The expression on her face reminded me very much of the old lady who lost her favourite slippers.

"He's not a bad bird," she said, lowering her voice in case feathery ears were listening. "But he has such strong views about things. And it's no good me arguing or being firm. He simply won't listen. I feel as though he's taken over my life completely, from morning to night."

"*Night night!*" squawked the parrot and shut his eyes. To my astonishment, Aunt Margaret drew the curtains and switched off the lights, beckoning me to follow her into the kitchen.

"I have to do that," she explained. "When he wants to sleep, he wants to sleep, and he can't bear any noise or light. I haven't seen any of my favourite telly programmes all week. He likes to sleep in the living room, you see."

"But Cap'n Baggle used to take him up to bed with him, didn't he?" I asked, thinking it would be more convenient for Aunt Margaret's programmes.

She shuddered. "I did that the first night," she said, "and the comments he made about my nightclothes were hardly fit to hear. I hate to think what he'll tell the captain. It's a sorry thing when a woman can't feel at home in her own house. He interferes with everything I do. And do you know, he tore my favourite slippers to shreds, squawking "*Old, old, old!*" I tried to pull them away from him, but he was so determined. I mean, I *liked* those old slippers!"

I looked at Aunt Margaret. She looked at me. All of a sudden, a pink flush spread up from her neck to the roots of her hair.

"Oh!" she said. There was nothing else to say, really.

Aunt Margaret looked after Perkins Parrot for another six weeks, until Cap'n Baggle came out of hospital and settled back in his old home.

"You've obviously taken great care of him," said the captain, rubbing Perkins' beak. "I've never seen him looking better."

"Is there anything I can do to help you, Captain?" asked Aunt Margaret. "Of course, I won't interfere unless you ask me."

The captain looked up with a smile. "I've never seen you looking better either, Margaret," he said with a grin. "Why don't you wear turquoise more often? From what Perkins tells me…"

But Aunt Margaret was hurrying me out of the house.

"We mustn't linger," she said. "I'm sure the captain values his independence. What are you smiling at, child?"

Mr. Ribble
and the
Rabbit

Deep in the country, thirty miles from the nearest town, lived a man who loved to garden. Every day, whether it was rainy or sunny, he was outdoors, tending to his plants. He worked hard from dawn to dusk to make sure that everything was as perfect as it could be.

But gardeners who like things to be perfect have a hard time. They can dig lots of smelly stuff into the soil to make it rich and fertile. They can pull out any weed that dares to push its leaves above the soil. They can mow and prune and trim. But they can't control the weather.

The man in this story, whose name was Mervyn Ribble, leapt out of bed every morning and threw back the curtains to see what the weather was like. If it was warm and sunny, he groaned. His lettuces needed some rain. If it was cloudy and wet, he moaned. His seedlings needed the sun. He was never satisfied. He felt as if he waged war on the weather day in and day out. But still, he loved to garden, and the pleasure he felt in seeing plants grow and being part of the turning of the seasons was worth any amount of difficulty. Year after year, Mr. Ribble worked on.

That was before he met the rabbit.

One fine spring day, when the garden was full of little green shoots and it felt as if the whole world was growing, Mr. Ribble went to look at some particularly fine plants he had set out the week before. He found them. At least, he found some stubby bits of stalk. The leaves had been munched and munched very thoroughly.

Mr. Ribble looked in horror at his precious plants. Something had eaten them, of that there could be no doubt. But what? Suddenly, the gardener felt eyes upon him. Looking up, he saw two bright little eyes staring back at him in a way that could only be described as cheeky. Sitting a few metres away, far enough for a quick getaway, was a small brown rabbit with long brown ears and a twitchety nose. There could be no doubt now about who was partial to plants.

Mr. Ribble waved his arms and made loud noises. The rabbit looked at him for a long minute, clearly thinking he had gone completely mad, before turning and lolloping slowly away.

With dread in his heart, Mr. Ribble walked around his garden looking for other signs of a rabbit on the rampage. He found plenty. The rabbit had obviously had a very good supper, an excellent breakfast, and several midnight snacks in the twelve hours since Mr. Ribble had last made his rounds. Mr. Ribble had to sit down on a handy bench to calm himself. He was a peaceful man, but he found a great hatred growing within him, and it was aimed at creatures with long ears, twitchety noses and little fluffy tails. His war with the weather paled in comparison with the battle with a bunny that now obsessed him.

Back in his little cottage, Mr. Ribble consulted his gardening books. He had hundreds of them, but he discarded the ones about bamboos and beeches and concentrated instead on a selection with titles such as *Pests in Your Garden* and *Garden Problems: Some Answers.*

Mr. Ribble was still reading at lunchtime. He found very little comfort in his books. The list of plants that rabbits did *not* like eating was dishearteningly short. The list of plants that rabbits were fond of went on for pages and pages, and contained all Mr. Ribble's favourites.

The advice about dealing with the pesky creatures was also very far from encouraging. Most of it involved wire-netting in some form, a thing Mr. Ribble hated to see in his garden. Alternatively, said the books, rabbits could be dealt with in a permanent way. This had a sinister ring to it, and as Mr. Ribble read on, he found that his fears had been right. The books suggested actions against rabbits that were not in the least bit friendly. Most of them involved bullets or substances not designed to improve a rabbit's digestion. Mr. Ribble instinctively shrank from these ideas. He spent his life encouraging living things. He really did not feel that he could be responsible for making sure that other living things stopped ... well, *living*.

In one of the books, there was a sentence that Mr. Ribble scarcely noticed on a first reading. It was, however, a very important sentence. It said, "Remember, rabbits rarely live alone." On a second reading of the chapter, this sentence hit Mr. Ribble between the eyebrows. If there is one thing that everyone knows about rabbits, it is that they have large families. Very large families. Mr. Ribble had a ghastly vision of a garden as full of rabbits as of plants. It was horrible.

For the first time in months, Mr. Ribble felt too depressed to garden for

the rest of the day. He took himself into town and tried to forget his troubles by having his hair cut (long overdue) and buying a new pair of boots.

Have you any idea how many reminders of rabbits there are in the average town? Poor Mr. Ribble found rabbit-shaped items everywhere. If he had thought for a moment, he would have remembered that Easter was only a week or two away. Shops were full of models of the Easter bunny, hopping merrily along with a basket of brightly coloured Easter eggs. Mr. Ribble saw only a world filled with rabbits. By the time he was ready to go home again, his nerves were in shreds. He couldn't face his usual evening stroll, but went to bed early, in the vague hope that it might all prove to be a horrible dream.

Next morning, Mr. Ribble awoke feeling refreshed and ready to tackle the

day. Sometime in the night his courage
had returned. He jumped straight out of
bed and ran to the telephone to order a
huge roll of wire-netting. He must, he felt,
be a match for a bunny, however cunning.
Over breakfast, Mr. Ribble finalized his
anti-rabbit plans. He had decided on a
multi-pronged attack.

The first essential, he knew, for any great general was to reconnoitre. Creeping quietly among his plants, Mr. Ribble scanned the garden with binoculars. He was determined to know his enemy.

It wasn't very long before Mr. Ribble spied a fluffy-tailed individual in his new vegetable patch, nonchalantly munching some young turnip tops. Remembering what the book had said, he ranged his binoculars over the whole area, expecting

at any moment to see several more bright-eyed browsers. The turnip-taster seemed to be alone. Nevertheless, Mr. Ribble could not be sure that the others were not hiding or nibbling at some other delicacy elsewhere in the garden. At the same time, he was pretty sure that the rabbit he had spotted was the same one he had seen the day before.

Mr. Ribble roamed his large garden, looking for more rabbits. There was none to be seen. He did, however, fall over a tree root and find something much more exciting. When Mr. Ribble had picked himself up and removed leaves and twigs from his clothes and his ears, he realized that he had not, in fact, tripped over a root. He had caught his foot in a hole. It was, he decided, almost certainly a hole in which a long-eared interloper might have made his home.

Mr. Ribble felt considerably cheered. Here, at last, was something he could do to improve matters. He hurried home and came back with a wheelbarrow full of rocks and stakes. In a very short time, he had filled the hole with the rocks and hammered stakes across the entrance. The welcome mat was no longer out for the rascally rabbit.

Mr. Ribble crept back to the new vegetable patch and peered around. There was no sign of the rabbit. Well, that's not actually true. There were lots of signs of the rabbit—chewed leaves, chewed stalks, chewed roots—but there was no rabbit. Mr. Ribble hoped very much that the creature had already found his home shut up for the summer and hopped it.

The wire-netting arrived in the afternoon. Mr. Ribble helped the truck driver to unload a huge roll of it. Then he

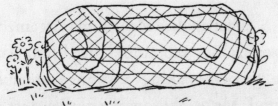

set to work at once to make rabbit-proof shelters for some of his favourite plants.

Of course, when Mr. Ribble went to put the wire cages in position, he found that some of the favourite plants were already tucked up in the rabbit's tummy. He gritted his teeth and positioned the other cages. They did not look attractive. They did not delight the eye in any way. But at least what was inside them was safe. Mr. Ribble felt he had done a good day's work.

That night, Mr. Ribble dreamed of an enormous rabbit. It chased him across the garden making a strange chuckling sound. Mr. Ribble awoke with a start and thew on his dressing gown. He pulled on his boots over his pyjamas and set off just as he was to see what had happened.

It was wonderful! Every single one of the plants protected by the wire-netting cages was still intact. They still didn't look attractive. They still didn't delight the eye. But the plants were safe, and that was the main thing.

Next morning, Mr. Ribble found that elsewhere in the garden, things were not so rosy. Several more plants had met the fangs of doom. Worse still, the hole among the tree roots was once more open for occupation. Someone—and it wasn't very hard to guess who—had politely removed the stakes and laid them in a neat pile on the grass. He had also removed the

rocks and placed them in rows along a nearby bank. Mr. Ribble, who was a gardener to his fingertips, had mixed feelings. He was appalled, of course, to find the rabbit once more in residence, but the carefully placed rocks had given him an idea for a shady rock garden. The arrangement of rocks was perfect. All he had to work out now was the planting. Mr. Ribble sat down at once to make his plans, completely forgetting in his excitement the rabbit problem only a short distance to his right.

That afternoon, Mr. Ribble rushed off to the nearest garden centre and bought some wonderful plants. Back at home, he planted them among the rocks along the bank. The plants were small, so the full effect was not yet visible, but Mr. Ribble felt confident that this would be a most successful experiment. It was true  that the cage of wire-netting over the bed rather spoilt the effect, but Mr. Ribble had enough sense not to take risks on the rabbit's own doorstep.

It was dusk before Mr. Ribble had finished his new project. Once again, he went to bed in a better frame of mind. He did not dream of rabbits at all, although at one point he did feel as if he was trapped inside a wire-netting cage. It wasn't at all pleasant, but

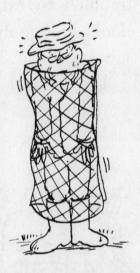

at least it didn't have big yellow teeth.

Next morning, Mr. Ribble checked first on his wire cages. They were fine. Then he hurried to his new shady rock garden. It took him a few moments to realize that something very strange had happened there.

The wire-netting cage had been carefully removed, and at first Mr. Ribble fully expected that his plants would be nibbled to extinction. But the plants looked fine, only—they had been moved!

Mr. Ribble sat down. The plants had been moved very carefully and patted back into the soil by experienced paws. What was more, Mr. Ribble had enough sense to realize that the new positions were much, much better than his first attempt. Someone who really knew about plants had made the changes. It surely could not be a certain local plant-fancier with a twitchety nose, could it? The idea seemed impossible, but Mr. Ribble's other ideas—that a wandering gardener had hopped over the fence and done a little replanting in the night, or that he himself had started sleepwalking and gardening while unconscious—were even more unlikely. Mr. Ribble sat on the bank with a thoughtful look on his face.

Ten minutes later, as Mr. Ribble still sat in the shade and puzzled, a little brown head popped out of the ground less than a metre away. Man and rabbit looked at each other for a long time. Mr. Ribble found himself making a decision. Plant-destroyers were the scum of the earth and should be firmly discouraged, but fellow gardeners deserved respect. Mr. Ribble gestured at the replanted bank.

"Very nice," he said.

"Thanks," said the rabbit.

Mr. Ribble rubbed his eyes. Then, on second thoughts, he rubbed his ears. Had he imagined it, or had the rabbit really spoken? There was only one way to find out.

"Is there anything else I should know about?" asked the gardener with short ears.

"You mean, did I eat anything else in the night?" asked the gardener with long ears. "No, I didn't. And I'm sorry about the other stuff, but I was so hungry when I got here. And I only ate things that you had lots of. I mean, when did you think you were going to eat all those turnips? Do you really like turnips?"

"Well, not a lot," confessed Mr. Ribble, "but I like growing them. What brought you here? Why, I mean, me?"

"I," cried the rabbit theatrically, "am an outcast. I was thrown out of my

old home because I peferred to plant things instead of nibbling them. It's not natural for a rabbit, you see."

"It wasn't in any of my gardening books, certainly," agreed Mr. Ribble, "but I'm always delighted to meet a fellow gardener. Er ... do you intend to stay?"

"I could be helpful," said the rabbit modestly. "I know a thing or two about plants, and burrowing can be useful for examining the soil. We could make a wonderful team, you and I."

Mr. Ribble admitted that this was true, but he felt it was necessary to draw up some, well, *ground* rules.

"I will grow you as many lettuces and other greens as you can eat," he said, "if you will promise not to nibble any of my other plants. Even turnips."

"It's a deal," said the rabbit.

"Holes in the ground, like this one, stay strictly among tree roots and similar. There will be no burrows in or under my lawns, flower beds or vegetable patch."

"Of course not," said the rabbit.

"Finally, you will not invite friends, relatives, strange rabbits or any other nibbling creature to join you in my garden. In fact, you will do your best to discourage any other animals with munching on their minds from coming into the garden."

"It will be my pleasure," said the rabbit, sounding very sincere.

"Then I look forward to a long and fruitful collaboration," said Mr. Ribble, extending his hand to shake a furry paw.

"Not so fast," replied the rabbit. "I also have a request that is very dear to my heart. If you are unable to grant it, I shall simply have to leave."

"Name it," said Mr. Ribble.

"Please," the rabbit couldn't help laughing, "no wire-netting. It looks dreadful!"

The
Ambitious
Hippo

The River Mlabu is sluggish and a bit slimy. It's not the kind of place you would choose for a swim. In the mud at the bottom of the lazily swirling water, squiggly things squirm and wiggly things worm. Under the banks, beneath the drip, drip of the grey-green moss, crocodiles sleep until they ... *snap!* It is not, for humans, a healthy area to linger. But it was precisely here that Hepzibah Hippo chose to raise her family.

Hepzibah and her Homer had only one child. As a result, they doted on their daughter, whose name was Helen.

"Just look at those jaws," said the fond father. "She could sink a thousand ships any day."

"And her bottom is *huge*!" said her proud mother. A big bottom is a thing of beauty to a hippo, who, to be truthful, never ever have small bottoms.

Helen Hippo glowed beneath her parents' praise. Loved and cherished from the moment she was born, she was not lacking in confidence. Her parents were keen to encouraged her to believe that anything was possible.

"Helen," they said, "when you grow up, you can be anything you want to be. All you have to do, darling, is believe in yourself and work hard. The sky's the limit. You are an amazing animal and a quite exceptional hippo. We feel sure that you will go far."

Helen Hippo was happy to hear all this. She believed every word of it. The only thing she had to do, she felt, was to work out what exactly she wanted to do. After that, actually doing it was a mere technicality.

For the first few years of her life, Helen was happy to wade and wallow. Things that squiggled and wiggled at the bottom of the river suffered badly under her fat little feet. Things that slept and snapped by the bank got tired of being bashed and barged when Helen heaved her great bulk out of the water every so often. Even the elephants that occasionally came to the river to drink steered clear of playful Helen. She once chomped into a dangling trunk, thinking it was a water snake, and elephants, as you know, have very long memories (especially when their trunks are a little short).

Helen, fortunately, was blissfully unaware that she was not the most popular animal in the area.

As Helen grew older (and heavier), she began to think it was time she had some ideas about what she would do with her life. Unfortunately, she was so very confident that these ideas were never in the least bit realistic.

Helen's first great passion was for dancing. She had seen graceful giraffes loping rhythmically over the plain. She had watched gazelles gambolling and prancing. Her mind was made up. She would be the greatest dancer in Africa—graceful, light-footed and untiring.

Three crushed frogs and a squashed warthog later, Helen was still convinced that her pirouettes were perfect and her leaps were legendary. To do her justice, she did practise at every opportunity. At first, her parents tried to encourage her.

"That was delightful, darling," they said, coughing as great clouds of dust were blown into their eyes by Helen's fiendish footwork. "It's wonderful to see so much … *enthusiasm!*"

"Look!" cried Helen. "I can stand on tiptoes. Look! Oh … oh … oh … I'm losing my balance … *crash!*"

Helen's father was speechless. You would be speechless too if a large hippo landed on you.

"I'm going to try that again," said Helen, gamely lumbering to her feet and ignoring the pathetic wheezing and whimpering coming from her father.

After that, Hepzibah and Homer tended to keep clear when Helen was cavorting. They felt that they could see perfectly well from a distance.

To tell the truth, most of the local animals kept clear at such times. The snappy crocodiles swam out to the middle of the river, with only their eyes and noses showing above the murky water.

The warthogs hid behind bushes.

Even the elephants stood behind trees and tried to pretend they weren't there. It was hard to pretend with the earth shaking and the trees trembling from the force of Helen's hopping and skipping. Several wildebeest decided to set off early on their great trek northwards.

Helen might be crashing around the undergrowth to this day if she had not suddenly decided to take up medicine instead. It is hard to say where she got the idea from, but its results were even worse for the other animals.

Hippo feet are no more designed for delicate work with a syringe than they are for dancing. Helen was forced to use more vigorous methods to make her patients well again.

She chased an unfortunate flamingo around for several hours because she said he looked flushed. It took several more hours for her mother to persuade her that flamingos are naturally pink.

When Helen found a large snake groaning after a huge meal, she decided that there was only one way to deal with the enormous lump in his tummy. She jumped up and down on him. That snake has never been the same since.

When Homer Hippo found himself suffering from ingrowing toenails, he felt obliged to encourage his medical daughter by letting her nibble them away. Now, hippo teeth are designed for mighty munching and huge chomping. There is nothing careful or delicate about them. Poor Homer did not walk again for weeks. Helen bandaged his feet with the largest leaves she could find and was very disappointed when her father refused to undergo further treatment. Even fathers have their limits.

Setbacks like these—let's not even discuss the porcupine who lost his quills or the giraffe with a sore throat and the truly disastrous treatment they received from a hopeful hippo doctor—eventually persuaded Helen to think of another career. She decided to be a great writer.

Of course, hippos can't actually *write*, so what she really meant was that she would be a great storyteller, but she thought that *writer* sounded better. There is a great and noble tradition of story-telling among hippos. It was a career that her parents were, once again, very happy to encourage.

"This will be much more suitable," Hepzibah told her husband as he hobbled around on his healing toes. "I mean, how can she go wrong? Even if she is not the greatest storyteller in the world, she can't do anyone any physical *damage*."

Homer gave a hearty snort of relief. This was, indeed, much more suitable. Sadly, they were both wrong.

Now, you may feel that this story is lacking in pace and humour. You may not like the characters or the setting. You may have taken note of my name on the title page and made a firm and fervent decision never to read another book of mine as long as you live. But I can tell you (and I would have my hand on my heart if it wasn't tapping away at the computer keys) that this story is a heart-stopping helter-skelter of thrills and excitement compared with Helen's hippo tales. To say that her stories were boring hardly covers the stultifying sleepiness they caused.

A whole herd of gazelles drifted into a coma when Helen told her favourite story: *The Hippo and the Dung Heap.* Those that later woke up found that their numbers were much reduced. I'm afraid that several crafty lionesses had found that lurking on the edge of Helen's story circle was a much more efficient way of hunting than all the creeping and crouching and pouncing they usually did. Really, an unconscious gazelle is the lion equivalent of a fast-food outlet.

Before very long, several vultures joined Helen's sessions. She was impressed that she was drawing such a varied audience. The vultures, I'm afraid, grew so fat that they could hardly fly.

A few weeks later, after the most unfortunate disappearance of several more gazelles, wildebeest, famingos and a baby elephant, a deputation from each group of animals (vegetarians only) arrived to speak to Hepzibah and Homer Hippo, who had not quite realized the full extent of the problem. (Well, they were asleep most of the time for obvious reasons, so they could hardly have been expected to notice.) They were surprised to see so many animals walking purposefully towards them.

"Mr. and Mrs. Hippo, this can't go on," said the largest elephant, who had been elected to speak. He was one of the few animals bigger and heavier than Homer and Hepzibah.

"This really is dreadful. We had no idea," cried the poor parents when the whole ghastly story was explained to them. "But how are we to persuade Helen to stop? She's ... er ... a strong-willed girl and very determined in all her many career choices."

"My friend the wildebeest here has a suggestion," boomed the elephant. "And I must say we all think it is a good one."

The wildebeest snickered with pride. "I knew your daughter would be reluctant to give up her storytelling," he said, "so I tried to think of a place where it wouldn't matter if listening animals went to sleep. It was very difficult, as some of us are in danger wherever we lay down our heads. But I suddenly had an inspiration. What about … the river?"

"The river?" For a moment, the hippo parents were puzzled. "But there's nothing in the river except squiggly things and wiggly things and crocodiles."

"Exactly," said the wildebeest. "Do we mind if anything happens to them?"

There was a short silence. Then…

"*Nah!*" chorused the elephant, the hippos, the flamingo, the gazelle and the warthog.

The next morning at breakfast, Homer played his part.

"How lucky all the animals are to be able to appreciate your talents, Helen," he said, "but sometimes I think it is a shame to entertain the privileged when there are so many creatures among us that need our help more urgently."

"Help?" Helen hadn't qutie lost her doctor's zeal for helping people whether they wanted it or not.

"I'm thinking of the poor crocodiles," said Homer, shaking his head sadly.

Helen was surprised. "Poor" and "crocodiles" were not words that were usually heard together. In fact, she had never heard her father have a good word to say about crocodiles before. Although she had never paid much attention to those creatures herself, she had heard some very nasty stories from the other

animals (in the days when she let them get a word in edgeways). It had not occurred to her that crocodiles were in any way unfortunate.

"Just imagine," sighed Homer, wiping an imaginary tear from his eye, "what it must be like to be hated by everyone you meet. No wonder they lurk under the mossy bank. What else can they do, shunned by society and condemned to hide away from the world? If only some exceptional animal could bring a little life and colour into their drab existence. Sometimes I can't sleep at nights for thinking about it."

Helen, who had been woken by her father's vigorous snoring since she was a baby hippo, should have been suspicious at this point, but there is no one so single-minded as an artist who wants an audience.

"I can do it!" she cried. "I can bring joy to a dark world! I can bring light to a life without hope! I can bring happiness to a sad, gloomy existence!"

"Steady on!" said her father, without thinking. "I mean, please, please, dear daughter, don't overtax yourself. An artistic temperament like yours can be a delicate thing, my dear."

"There's no need to worry about me," said Helen cheerfully (and with accuracy). She took her artistic temperament off to the riverbank at once.

Well, the rest, as they say, is history. The poor crocodiles, at first deeply puzzled by a hippo who began droning on in the middle of the river, soon found themselves strangely fascinated. A little later, they all found themselves drowsy. Before long, each one of them was floating lazily, eyes shut, without a thought in the world of going ... *snap!*

With the crocodiles safely asleep, and Helen still droning interminably on, the other animals jumped in with a splash. They had a wonderful time, and the poor crocodiles slept through all of it. While deep on the bottom of the river, the wiggly things and the squiggly things didn't worm or squirm at all. They simply slept.

Lucy
Had a
Little Goat

Lucy lived on a farm. She liked all the animals but she knew that they had jobs to do. The cows gave milk early in the morning, long before Lucy was up, and in the afternoon. The hens laid eggs whenever they felt like it, but Lucy's mother collected them twice a day. The sheep had woolly coats that were sheared once a year. These animals didn't have individual names, and Lucy didn't think of them as pets.

Some other animals on the farm did have names. In the big barn, there lived three cats called Eeny, Meeny and Mo. Lucy's mother had told her that they were called that because she couldn't decide which to choose from the kittens of the last old cat and had ended up keeping all three of them. They ran about and caught all the mice they could, but they didn't come into the house.

Dad's dog Jip didn't come into the house, either, unless he wasn't well. He worked with Dad when he was looking after the sheep and was really clever at dealing with the silly sheep.

Lucy didn't think of the cats and the dog as pets either. They were just part of the busy life on the farm.

But when Lucy was old enough to go to school, she soon found that other children thought about their animals in a different way.

"I've got a hamster," said Tommy proudly. He sleeps a lot but at night he runs around and around on his little wheel. It's a bit squeaky. His name is Harry."

"Why do you have him?" asked Lucy. She had never heard of hamsters but she thought maybe they laid eggs or something. Although she couldn't really see the hens on the farm running around in a little wheel.

Tommy looked surprised. "He's a pet," he said. "I have him so that I can look after him and play with him."

Lucy understood about farming but she didn't really understand about pets.

"And then you eat him, I suppose," she said, matter of factly.

Tommy burst into tears and went to tell the teacher that Lucy was a horrible girl who wanted to eat his hamster. The teacher looked sharply at Lucy but said, "Oh no, Tommy, I'm sure that's not true. She knows that you love Harry. Have you asked her about her pets?"

Lucy frowned. "I help to take care of cows and sheep and hens," she said, "but I don't play with them and they don't have little wheels to run around."

That evening, the teacher had a word with Lucy's mother when she came to collect her. And when Lucy was tucked

up in bed much later, she read her a story about a little boy who had a pet rabbit. She explained to Lucy that children who didn't have animals around them all the time, as Lucy did, often liked to have an animal of their own at home.

"I wouldn't want a rabbit," said Lucy sleepily. "There are hundreds of them out in the field. And anyway, do they *like* being shut up like that?"

"Well, I don't know about that," said her mother. "I expect they like being looked after."

But Lucy was already asleep and dreaming of rabbits running around and around on little wheels.

Lucy didn't say much about it, but over the next few weeks she often thought about pets. She was still pretty puzzled about it. Another little boy at school had some fish in a tank. Lucy could see that it might be nice to stroke and feed a rabbit, who might wrinkle his nose in a cute way and look as if he was enjoying a lettuce leaf you had brought him. But what was the point of having fish? You couldn't stroke them. You couldn't tell if they were pleased to see you. Lucy shook her head. She couldn't understand it at all. She even wondered if perhaps they tasted good, but after the hamster incident she knew better than to ask.

Gradually, Lucy came to realize that almost *all* the children in the class had pets. One day in maths, the children had to cut out animals and put them on a chart to show which was the most popular pet. Most of Lucy's friends were cutting out cats and dogs and other small furry animals. Lucy decided against trying to cut out huge numbers of cows and sheep and hens. Anyway, she didn't think they counted. She cut out a picture of Jip instead and explained that he was her Dad's dog. That seemed to make everyone happy. Tommy, who hadn't spoken to her since the day they had discussed hamsters, sat next to her and helped her stick her picture on the chart.

That evening after supper, Lucy told her mother that she needed to have a pet.

"People like you better if you do," she explained.

"That's silly," said her mother, "but you can have a pet if you like. Only you will have to look after it all by yourself. We're too busy looking after the other animals to help. And remember, it's really important to look after animals properly. You know how Daddy feels about that."

"I will look after it," said Lucy. "Can we buy one this weekend?"

"Not this weekend, darling," said her mother. "We're going to the County Show, remember? Next weekend we will think about it."

But Lucy simply couldn't get pets off her mind, and perhaps that is why although three members of the family went to the County Show, four members came back. The newcomer was a goat!

"Are you sure, sweetheart?" Lucy's dad had asked. "This little chap is very young, but goats get big. You won't be able to bring him in the house."

"I know. That's okay," said Lucy. "I just think he has a little tiny bit of all the animals I like best in him. He's black and white like the cows. His face is a little bit like a sheep's. And he's got bright little eyes like the hens."

So that was that.

"And I'm going to call him Gordon," said Lucy. She couldn't understand why her mother and father burst out laughing, even when they said they knew someone called Gordon themselves.

"Anyone would be glad to share a name with my Gordon," she said.

Over the next few weeks, Lucy's dad suggested several new names for her Gordon, and not all of them were polite.

"Guzzler, would be a better name," he said. "Or Greedyguts. Or Gulper. Or Gorger. Or, wait a minute, what about Gobbler?"

"It's natural for a young goat to be hungry," said Lucy. "Gordon is growing."

Gordon certainly was growing. But he was also a guzzler, a gorger, a gulper, a gobbler and a greedyguts. He ate anything he could reach, from Lucy's mother's old gardening gloves, left on the fence, to half of one of her father's boots, left outside to dry. As for the flowers and shrubs that struggled to grow around the farmhouse, their struggle was over. Gordon ate them, and that was that.

When Gordon attacked the laundry, flapping in the breeze one sunny morning, Lucy's mother put her foot down.

"That goat has to be kept further away from the house," she said. "We will tether him in the orchard. You can move him each day so that he always has fresh new grass to munch. He will be happy and our underwear will be safe."

Gordon was certainly very happy in the orchard. The grass was delicious there. But Gordon soon found other ways of getting food. He realized that if he butted the trees hard with his head (and his head was extremely hard), little green apples and plums and pears would tumble down. Gordon didn't mind that they were green, but as time passed and the fruit began to ripen, he enjoyed it even more. And it seemed to fall off much more easily, too.

One summer evening, Lucy's parents wandered out into the orchard to see how their crop was doing. Lucy went along too, to find out how Gordon was doing. The farmer and his wife searched high and low, but all they found were two very shrivelled apples that refused to fall from their branch, a rotten plum and three pears right at the top of their tree. It was all too clear who the culprit was. Gordon wasn't very good at his "Who? Me?" act.

"Well, it's too late now," said the farmer. "But we'll have to find a new home for him next year."

He meant that they must find another place for Gordon to be tethered, but Lucy, waiting discreetly behind a tree in case there was any shouting, heard this with horror. She thought her father meant Gordon must leave the farm. Right there and then she decided to hide him.

It's not easy to hide a goat. It's even more difficult to hide a hungry goat. That evening, when both her parents were inside the house, Lucy tried putting Gordon in the old stable. But next morning, when she crept out before breakfast to take him some cornflakes, she found that he had chewed through the rotting wood of the old door and was back in the flowerbeds doing his worst. Lucy hurriedly pulled him away and shut him in the big barn instead. It was a huge mistake. Let loose with dozens of sacks of grain, Gordon had a wonderful time.

By the end of the day, when a large chunk of a haystack, a bag of beans, some chickenfeed and a bucket of whitewash had all been consumed by Gordon in various hiding places, Lucy was convinced that there was nowhere on the farm to hide him safely. Perhaps that is why she had the outrageous idea of taking him to school.

School was not very far away, and Lucy was allowed to walk there by herself as she could go all the way along paths beside the fields of her own farm. The next morning, she set off earlier than usual, telling her mother that there was a special visitor at school that day.

"I know," said her mother rather unexpectedly. "I hope you like him. Have a good day!"

Lucy knew that she would never be able to smuggle Gordon unseen into school, but she hoped that she could pretend that she had brought him along to show her friends. Then maybe her teacher would let her leave him on the playing field until it was time to go home.

But things did not go according to plan. Because she had set off much earlier than usual, there was no one about when she came into the playground. The school caretaker had already opened the school and was busy doing something in his shed at the back, but there were no children in sight. Lucy was trying to decide what to do when the heavens opened and it began to rain heavily. Without thinking, she pulled open the door and pushed Gordon inside. Lucy had never been in the school when it was empty before. With Gordon by her side, she wandered down the long corridors and peeped into classrooms she didn't usually see. But all the while, in the back of her mind, she was wondering what to do about Gordon. He looked horribly conspicuous.

Suddenly, coming around the next corner, Lucy heard footsteps. Someone was here already, and from the heavy tread of the feet, it must be one of the teachers. Lucy panicked. She opened the nearest door and pushed Gordon inside, then strolled down the corridor trying to look as innocent as possible.

"Hello, Lucy, you're early today," said her teacher.

That morning, Lucy could hardly concentrate at all. She wondered what Gordon was doing. She wondered if he was safe. She had pushed him into one of the storerooms on the other side of the corridor, but it wasn't until morning break that several horrible thoughts struck her all at once. What, she wondered, if the storeroom didn't have a window? What if

it didn't have enough air? What if Gordon was suffocating?

Lucy knew that she had been very silly. She was almost in tears as she rushed up to her teacher and explained that her Gordon must be rescued at once.

It took ages for the teacher to start to understand what Lucy was saying.

"A goat?" he asked. "In a cupboard? Are you sure, Lucy?"

"Yes, yes!" It was clear from Lucy's distraught face that something was badly wrong. The teacher took hold of the little girl's hand and said gently, "Why don't you show me?"

Out in the corridor, Lucy stood with her teacher in front of the cupboard door. There was no sound from inside. Lucy hardly dared open the door. The teacher stretched out his hand and turned the knob.

There *was* a window inside! There was a goat, too, peacefully asleep on the floor. And there was the most dreadful mess you have ever seen. Half-eaten books were heaped all over the floor. There didn't seem to be one without nibbled pages or a huge chunk bitten out of the cover.

"Oh no!" wailed Lucy. "Oh Gordon, what have you done?"

"Did I hear my name?" asked an amused voice behind her.

Lucy and the teacher turned. The scene in the cupboard was horrifying, but this was worse. Standing there with expressions of astonishment were the headmaster and a strange man—a Very Important Visitor who was being shown around the school.

"Mr. Miles," said the headmaster, "I can assure you that this sort of thing has *never* happened before. I know that you would not want to make the generous donation you are suggesting if you thought that we allowed *this* sort of thing. I promise you…"

But the man was bending down and smiling broadly.

"I think you must be Lucy," he said. "And I'm very much afraid this must be my namesake, Gordon. Your parents told me that you had chosen an excellent name for your goat!"

"Well, shall we…?" The headmaster was still trying to smooth over the situation.

But Gordon Miles was laughing as Gordon the goat, hearing the noise, woke up and at once started chewing a copy of *Transport Through the Ages*. It didn't, however, seem to appeal to him very much, for he dropped it at once and began on *Five Hundred Famous Physicians*.

"These books appear to appeal to goats as much as to children," said the Very Important Visitor. "I think I'll have to increase my donation to cover what Gordon here has saved you the trouble of throwing away. Now, Lucy, why don't I help you take him home?"

The
Impossible
Pony

From the age of three, Emilia Estefan wanted a pony. She had a toy one with a pink mane and a blue tail, which she brushed and braided every day. She asked her father for a purple pony with a yellow mane and an orange tail. Her father said that he doubted very much if such a thing existed, and that if it did, it should be put out of its misery right away. Emilia didn't understand what he was talking about, but she knew that it meant no. She turned her head away when her father came to say goodnight and wouldn't speak to him for a week. Emilia's mother tried to improve matters by making her a very special birthday cake—in the shape of a pony (purple, of course) with a yellow mane and an orange tail. Emilia's father laughed when he saw it and said that this was one pony he would be very glad to help put out of its misery.

Emilia had lots of lovely presents for her birthday. One of them was a toy pony with its very own stable. It wasn't purple. It was brown with a blond mane and tail, its own saddle and bridle, and a little bucket with a real handle for its feed. Emilia looked at it for about three seconds and threw it to the back of her cupboard. She didn't think a brown pony was pretty at all.

A few months later, Emilia had her first proper riding lesson. She was a little surprised to find that none of the ponies were pink or purple or yellow. In fact, most of them *were* brown. But the smallest pony of all was a beautiful creamy colour with a darker mane and tail. Emilia fell in love with Sugar on the spot and started being extra nice to her father from that moment on. Christmas, she knew, was not very far away.

When Emilia came to write her Christmas list, she found it very easy. She had already learnt to write her own name but not very much else, so she dictated the list to her mother and begged her to use her very best handwriting so that Santa had absolutely no trouble in reading it.

"Put 'Emilia's list' at the very top," she told her mother.

"Aren't you forgetting something?" enquired Mrs. Estefan.

"You could underline it," suggested her daughter. "Or you could write it in red pen. I don't want him to make any mistakes."

"I was thinking that you might like to say 'please'," suggested the scribe, "or you may find that this list doesn't get written at all."

Emilia decided to get it all over in one go.

"Please, please, please, please, please, please, please," she said, "will you write this under my name: one creamy-coloured pony who looks just like Sugar, only I will call him Angel. One saddle for Angel. Two blankets for Angel. One bridle for Angel—a red one would be good. One stable with his name painted on the door. One feed bucket with his name on it. One thing for putting water in with his name on it. Lots of oats and those nobbly things they have at the riding stable. A brush for his coat. I think that should have his name on it, too. A vet to look after him when he's not very well. More riding lessons. A pink dress with sparkly bits on it."

Emilia's mother looked at the list.

"That last thing doesn't seem to fit with the rest," she said.

"No, you can leave it off, if you like," said Emilia. "I'd much rather have the other things. And I think I should sign my name, to show I really mean it."

She signed her name and, next time they were in the supermarket where there was a letterbox for messages to Santa Claus, her mother held Emilia up so she could post it.

That evening, Emilia's father sat down on the bed when he came to say goodnight.

"Goodnight, my dear, dear, nice daddy," said Emilia with a sweet smile.

"Cut it out, Em," said her father. "I know what this is about, and I can tell you now that there is no way you will have a pony for Christmas. I don't want you to be disappointed, sweetheart, but ponies are very, very expensive. You've only been learning to ride for a month and you might go off the whole idea before the end of January. Need I remind you about Rufus the rabbit?"

Emilia had pleaded and begged for Rufus only a year before. About a week after Christmas, when her mother had given her some cabbage leaves to take out to Rufus, Emilia had mentioned quite

casually that she was not very interested in rabbits any longer and would rather have a hamster. Eventually, Rufus went to a good home in the next village. Mr. and Mrs. Estefan shut their ears to all future mentions of hamsters.

Now, lying in bed, Emilia tried patiently to explain to her father that the question of Angel was very different from the question of Rufus.

"He was a rabbit," she said clearly, as if talking to a very small child, "and Angel will be a pony. It's a completely different animal. Anyone can see that."

"Yes, I can see that," said her father grimly, "but it doesn't matter. You are not old enough to have a pony of your own and that's the end of it. You'd better think of some more things like the pink dress to go on your list. If not, Santa may not bother to come at all. It's a long journey to make from the North Pole to bring just one dress."

Emilia scowled and sulked. She didn't want to add anything else to her list because she didn't want to give Santa the impression that anything else would do. However, about a week before Christmas, she began to worry that this was a high-risk strategy. Her faithful scribe wrote out a new list, which was the same as the old one but twice as long. This, too, was posted in the supermarket.

Secretly, Emilia still hoped for the surprise arrival of Angel on Christmas morning. But as she opened present after present and found that she had almost *all* the other things on her list, hope began to fade.

She left all her beautiful new toys and clothes in a heap under the tree and pulled out the old brown-pony-and-stable toy from the back of the cupboard. The pony was still the wrong colour, but it was better than nothing.

Six months later, when Emilia's fifth birthday came around, she had become really good at riding. Her teacher said she had natural talent, and Emilia's parents began to wonder if, after all, she shouldn't in the future have a pony of her own. But not yet. She was only five, and when she started school next term, she would be far too busy to think about riding.

Emilia opened her birthday presents and found, once again, that there was no pony. She felt like throwing the presents on the floor and stamping on them, but several of them were interesting books about ponies, so she decided not to.

A few weeks later, however, school turned out to be much more interesting than she had feared. She soon became friends with five other little girls who were just as mad about ponies as she was. Two of them already had ponies of their own. The others were waging campaigns very like Emilia's on their parents. She picked up several very useful tips from them for putting on further pressure.

Maybe it was the pressure. Maybe it was the fact that she was older now, but shortly before Christmas that year, her father asked her to get into the car to make a special surprise journey. Emilia, thinking it was a pre-Christmas visit to some dreadful aunt or boring cousin, moaned and groaned and took as long as she could to put her coat and gloves on. Then she pretended she couldn't find her boots.

"Well, if you don't want to go and choose a pony today, we don't have to," said her father.

The boots miraculously appeared, and Emilia was in the car almost before her father had finished his sentence.

"We're going to see a pony that was advertized in the paper," explained her father. "It isn't exactly the colour you wanted, but apart from that it sounds just right for you. Let's see what we think when we get there. If we don't like it, we can wait until another suitable one comes up for sale."

Emilia didn't much like the sound of waiting. She had given up caring what colour the pony was long ago. Now she was desperate to be the third member of her group of friends to own her own pony. She couldn't believe her luck.

The farm where the pony was being kept was shabby and untidy.

"It looks as though they've fallen on hard times," said Mr. Estefan. "I expect that's why they need to sell."

A man with a lot of very white teeth met them at the gate.

"So pleased to meet you," he said with a broad smile. "My name is Metcalf. Come right this way. Oh, sorry, please mind the mud."

Mr. Estefan shook his shoe and tried not to think about the squelchy feeling around his toes as they followed Mr. Metcalf into the yard. On the other side of it, a pony was looking at them over its stable door. It had a black face with a white blaze on its forehead and whinied in a friendly way to the visitors.

"I love him," said Emilia at once. "Please can I have him, Dad?"

"First things first, sweetheart," said Mr. Estefan, trying to sound as if he knew what he was talking about. "Let's find out a bit more about him first. What is his name, Mr. Metcalf?"

"Dorinda," said the man, with yet another huge smile.

"Dorinda? That's an unusual name for a … oh! it's a *she*!" laughed Emilia's father, patting the pony gingerly on the nose and withdrawing his hand quickly when the pony took a quick nip at his driving gloves.

"Just her way of saying hello," said Mr. Metcalf. "What would you like to know, sir … and madam?"

Once again, Mr. Estefan tried to sound businesslike. He pulled out a pencil and notebook and began to ask questions.

"Age?"

"She'll be five in January," said the owner promptly, "and she's the sweetest-natured little lass you could hope to find. She'll suit your daughter down to the ground, I can assure you."

"How is her health?" asked Mr. Estefan briskly.

Mr. Metcalf seemed to be examining the door frame with great care.

"I've never had a day's trouble with her," he said. "We haven't called the vet to her in all the time we've had her."

"And you're selling her because...?" asked the prospective buyer delicately.

Mr. Metcalf managed to smile and sigh at the same time.

"It breaks our hearts," he said, "but my little girl is just too big for Dorinda now. We don't think it's fair to keep her just as a pet. She loves to be ridden."

Mr. Estefan made a few more enquiries, but Mr. Metcalf glanced once or twice at his watch.

"I'm sorry," he said, "but I don't like to be away from my wife for too long." He did his smiling-and-sighing trick again. "She's very ill," he said, "and she worries if I leave her alone for more than an hour."

Mr. Estefan felt dreadful for taking so much time.

"Well, I don't pretend to be an expert," he said. "We'll arrange for our vet to come and have a look at Dorinda as soon as we can. She did say that she could come out here tomorrow morning or on Friday, whichever is more convenient."

"Both would be absolutely fine," said Mr. Metcalf charmingly, "but I'm afraid you will be taking rather a risk. I have two more families coming out to see our Dory this afternoon. And if one of them makes me an offer…"

Emilia's father was a level-headed man, but he had heard more about ponies in the last few years than he could really stand. The idea of having to deal with Emilia's disappointment and start looking all over again made him completely lose his head. He bought the pony—without even being completely sure how many legs she had or whether they worked.

It had been decided that the new pony would be looked after by the riding stable until proper arrangements could be made at Emilia's home. The next morning, Emilia and her father were there bright and early to see the pony unloaded from her horsebox.

"Hello, Angel," cried Emilia with a big bag of apples in her arms.

Angel turned out to be anything but. It took four of the riding school staff, plus Emilia, plus her father, to persuade Angel to come out of her box. In the end, brute force was not enough. Only the offer of an apple for every tiny footstep persuaded the pony to edge her way out into the yard. The expression on her face, as she looked around at her new home, could only be described as unenthusiastic.

"It will take her some time to get used to it," said Emilia's father, hopefully.

"Hmm," the owner of the riding stable wasn't so sure. "Did you have the vet look at her?" she asked.

Mr. Estefan blushed, which was an answer in itself. The owner went inside to ring the vet at once. "Just to be on the safe side," she said.

Emilia and her father waited for the vet to arrive and tried hard not to look as anxious as they felt. When she did arrive, her examination seemed to take a very long time.

"Well," she said at last, "do you want the good news or the bad news?" Mr. Estefan groaned.

"Is she okay?" asked Emilia. "Is my Angel ill or something?"

"No, she's not ill," said the vet. "In fact, she's in remarkably good condition considering she hasn't been looked after very well. She's quite a bit older than you were told, though, and I'm afraid you won't be able to ride her for a while. Even then, she may need quite a bit of schooling. She's not a youngster and she may not take kindly to being taught new ways."

Emilia was so disappointed, she was almost in tears. But Mr. Estefan had caught a hint of something more cheerful in the vet's voice and looked up with a question in his eyes.

"The good news," said the vet, "is that she is going to be a mother quite soon. You've got two ponies for the price of one, Emilia!"

As a matter of fact, Emilia never did ride Angel, who decided there was no need for her ever to live up to her name. She lived happily in a meadow near the house and watched with pride the career of her daughter, Angelina. You see, a few years later, Emilia and that little cream pony with a dark mane and tail won every cup and ribbon and rosette for miles around!

Wilfred,
the
Wanderer

When Mrs. Worm asked her son what he wanted to be when he grew a little longer, he did not hesitate.

"I want to travel," he said. "I want to see the world."

Mrs. Worm was perplexed. She had never heard of a worm who wanted to move beyond the patch of earth he knew best. Travelling sounded dangerous. She decided that she must try to dissuade her son with all possible speed.

"I don't think you've thought this through, Wilfred," she said. "What about mountains?"

"What about them?" asked Wilfred.

"Well, they are usually made of rock. You are a strong little worm, but you can't burrow through solid rock. It would hurt your head."

"Then I'll go around," said Wilfred happily. "Where there are mountains, there must be valleys. We learnt about it in geography lessons."

Mrs. Worm frowned. So that was where all this was coming from. Wilfred had a young and dynamic geography teacher called Ms. Wanda Worm. She had clearly been filling his head with all kinds of crazy ideas.

"What about rivers, Wilfred?" asked his mother. "Some of them are very deep. You may not be able to go under them. What are you going to do about fast-flowing rivers?"

"I'll go around those as well," said Wilfred. "Rivers have to start somewhere, you know."

As a matter of fact, Mrs. Worm did not know. Education when she was a girl was not as thorough as Wilfred's up-to-date schooling.

"Hmmm," she said. "What about birds? Some of those foreign birds may be a lot trickier to avoid than the kind we have here. They might have much longer beaks, for one thing. Or extra-excellent hearing. What are you going to do if some great big monster-bird gets hold of you?"

"I'll wiggle," said Wilfred. "Or I might hold myself very straight, like this, and pretend to be a stick. It would depend. And I promise I will be very, very careful. I want to come home and tell you all about my adventures. It's no good if I get eaten halfway."

"No, no, indeed," said poor Mrs. Worm faintly. She could see it was no use arguing with Wilfred, so she settled herself down under the tulip bed to worry. It was what she did best. As a matter of fact, it's what most mothers do best.

Worms from miles around came to say goodbye to Wilfred when he set out on his great journey. They couldn't wave, of course, but in time-honoured worm fashion they sang, "For He's a Jolly Good Wiggler" and "Worms Meet Again" until the tip of his tail, squiggling in fine style, was out of sight.

"Well, that's the last we'll see of him," said old Wilberforce Worm, who was known to be a pessimist.

"Don't talk like that!" cried Mrs. Worm. "He has been most carefully brought up. He knows all the dangers and can look after himself. I think that the idea of young worms getting out and seeing a bit of the world before they settle down is an excellent one."

There's nothing like criticism from an ancient and depressing relative to make you suddenly enthusiastic about something!

Meanwhile, and much sooner than he had thought, Wilfred hit his first big problem. "Hit" is, in fact, exactly what he did. With a sickening thud, his nose came up against something that felt like a huge, solid, smooth-skinned worm. It was a gas pipe, actually, but Wilfred didn't know that and spent several hours trying to

engage the pipe in conversation. When he finally realized that he could simply burrow under it and wiggle on his way, he felt a little foolish. But, after all, one of his reasons for travelling was to learn from his varied experiences. He felt better when he thought of that.

You have probably heard of slow worms. Well, Wilfred was a quick worm. He was young and fit, and he squiggled and wiggled at a quite incredible speed. It was not long before he was a long way from home. Travelling, he decided, was very exciting, but it was a little bit lonely, too. He wished he had talked his brother Walter into coming with him, but Walter's interest was in building, not travelling. He aimed to be the first worm to build a thousand-burrow hotel.

Pretty soon, Wilfred became aware that the soil was changing. Very gradually, it stopped being dark brown and became light brown. A little while later, it became distinctly yellow. Before long, it was not only yellow but wet, and with a strong, salty taste that Wilfred found unpleasant. Wilfred felt his skin going flabby in the dampness. He didn't like it very much. Although he hated the idea of turning back, he didn't feel that burrowing through wet grit was much fun. When his tail was almost nipped by a kind of hinged contraption, lurking beside his tunnel, Wilfred decided it was time to make a strategic retreat. He was just in time.

As Wilfred turned to go back, the sand (of course, that was what he was in) suddenly became much, much wetter. The tide was coming in. Wilfred wiggled as he had never wiggled before. He was hugely relieved to find himself back in proper soil again, and what was more he recognized that he was travelling through cabbage roots. The smell and the touch of them, tickling his sides, gave Wilfred his first pang of homesickness. He curled up under a cabbage and went to sleep.

Grrrrmmmaphhhh! Wilfred was woken by a dreadful noise. The cabbages were being harvested by machine bright and early in the morning. Now Wilfred was a fast worm, but cabbage-picking machines are even faster. Before he knew what was happening, our worm felt his cabbage being torn from the ground, roots and all, and flung into a dark space full of hundreds of other cabbages.

Wilfred wound himself as tightly as he could around the cabbage roots. The machine was shuddering and juddering so much that it was hard to hang on. At last, just when he thought his last moment had

come, the jiggling stopped. Human voices
rang out, and strong hands picked up the
cabbage he clung to.

Now Wilfred had had mixed success
in his meetings with humans so far. As a
youngster, he found himself picked up by
a small child, who ran to her mother with
cries of joy. "Ook! Ook! Mummy! I gotta
snake! Sssssssss!"

Poor Wilfred, dangling
from the clutch of fat little
fingers, had no time to
feel offended. (Snakes,
as far as worms are
concerned, are huge,
uncivilized creatures
with no delicacy or
finesse. To be fair,
snakes are just as
rude and scathing
about worms.)

The toddler's mother's reply filled him with dread, however.

"Carrie, don't eat it!" she cried. "Put it down!"

Eat it? Wilfred had never heard of humans eating worms. Birds, yes. Toads, maybe. But humans? Yet here was a baby human opening her pink little mouth, in which a handful of tiny teeth gleamed white and sharp. Wilfred feared that he was doomed, but the next instant the mother of the child had seized him roughly (it took him weeks to recover from the bruizes) and flung him over into a flowerbed.

That was not a good experience, although it did teach Wilfred to avoid humans wherever possible. However, on another occasion, he was wiggling along, minding his own business, when a huge, sharp, metal thing suddenly sliced into the soil in front of him. He was being dug up! A second later, he lay on top of the soil, while the metal thing hovered above him, ready to smash him to smithereens. But the next thing he knew, a kindly and very wrinkled old face peered down at him and pushed him gently out of the way.

"Oh no, off you go little worm," it said. "You do so much good in my garden. I wouldn't want to hurt *you*."

Wilfred took the hint and quickly disappeared into the freshly-dug soil, where he found lots of delicious compost had been added.

All this is just to explain that when Wilfred, clinging to his cabbage, suddenly felt himself carried away by human hands, he had very mixed feelings.

"There you are," he heard a deep voice say, as the cabbage was dumped on to a table, "ready for supper."

"Can you cut up the cabbage for me, Harriet?" he heard another voice say. "Be very careful with the knife and make sure you wash it thoroughly in the big colander."

Wilfred didn't feel happy about the idea of knives or streams of water, so he decided that this might be the moment to make a quick getaway. Doing his best to pretend to be a spoon, he slithered off the

cabbage and set off across the kitchen table as quickly as he dared without drawing attention to himself. Spoons, after all, are not renowned for their turn of speed.

Wilfred was approaching the table edge and just beginning to wonder how he would cope with it, when a scream stopped him in his tracks.

"*Yeeeeeuuuch!*" cried the creature called Harriet. "A worm! Oh, somebody squish it! Quick!"

"Don't you dare!" shouted another voice. "It's just what I've been looking for. Give it to me!"

"I'm not touching it!" shrieked Harriet. "If you want it, you'll have to come and get it."

The voice that had warned about the sharp knife broke in again.

"James, what exactly do you want that worm for? You're not going to chop it up or do experiments on it or anything, are you?"

"No!" James sounded shocked. "I want it for my wormery. I've only got two worms in it at the moment, and they're not very big. This one will be much better."

"Oh, all right," said his mother. "But be careful how you handle it. Even worms deserve a bit of respect."

Wilfred warmed to this woman. To be fair, James was pretty careful. He picked Wilfred up very gently and carried him off to a contraption made of wood with a window in the front. Just before he

was dropped, Wilfred got a look at it. It was filled with layers of soil of different colours, and there were some nicely rotten leaves on the top. Wilfred landed with a plop on top of the leaves and lost no time in burrowing out of sight. He had no idea what was happening to him, although he felt quite safe after what the woman in the kitchen had said, and he felt excited that he already had amazing stories to tell his family when he returned home.

It was a strange world in which young Wilfred now found himself. In one way, it was just like being back in the soil again, and he could burrow to his heart's content as long as he went along or up and down. But the soil was only a few worms thick sideways. If he tried to bend in his burrowing, he hit a wooden or glass wall. It was all very odd. Wilfred stopped to think about it a bit.

"Excuse *me*, I'm trying to get past!" moaned a voice behind him. "Can't you burrow somewhere else? How did a big fat worm like you get in here anyway?"

"I'm not fat!" protested Wilfred. "I'm just well built. That's what my mother says, anyway. How did you come to be so weedy?"

"Weedy? How dare you!" The strange worm tried to look fierce and failed dismally.

Wilfred felt that he had not made a good start.

"Look," he said, "I don't mean to be unfriendly. It's just that this thing we're in seems to be a bit small for me. If I wiggle just a little bit off-course, I hit these wall things. I haven't found out how to get around them yet."

The new worm smirked. "Well, that's where being small is useful," he said. "I don't keep barging into things like you do. And I can tell you all about getting around these walls. I've been here a few weeks. You can't."

"Can't what?"

"Can't get around them! We're not underground. We're inside a thing that boy calls a wormery. There isn't any way of getting around it."

Wilfred remembered Ms. Wanda Worm's exciting and interesting geography lessons.

"There's always a way," he said. "Just leave it to me. Are you the only other worm in here? I'm Wilfred, by the way. What's your name?"

"Wayne," said the worm, "and I'm not alone. My sister Wilhemina is here too, but she doesn't like wiggling much so she just stays near the bottom."

"Doesn't like wiggling!" Wilfred, who lived to wiggle, was shocked. "Whatever's the

matter with you worms? I can see we're going to have to do a lot of work before we make our escape."

The other worms were no match for Wilfred. He took charge and they meekly followed. After a period of serious research, Wilfred discovered that Wayne was right. There was no way out of the wormery—except up and over the top.

And that would require excellent wiggling skills and a great deal of strength. There and then, Wilfred put Wayne and his sister on a fitness programme. They practised wiggling in all directions allowed by the wormery. Pretty soon, all those careful layers of soil were hopelessly mixed up. Wilfred hoped that the boy James wouldn't be cross about it.

On the contrary, young James was delighted. He decided to take the wormery to school to show his teacher. Wilfred, Wilhemina and Wayne were blissfully unaware of this as they busied themselves with strength and suppleness exercises.

It was, perhaps, unfortunate that Wilfred elected to attempt to lead his escape team at the very moment that thirty pairs of eyes were staring intently at the wormery, eager for signs of action.

"They've been moving like mad, honestly," explained James as his classmates gathered around. "I don't know where they are just at this minute. But if we're quiet, they might start moving again pretty soon."

Where "they" were was just under the surface of the soil, undergoing a final briefing from Wilfred. A moment later and James' prediction was fulfilled—and how! Three worms hurtled from the soil and hurled themselves at the glass sides of the wormery. Then, with incredible vigour, they starting to squirm up the wooden and glass sides.

"*Oooooooooh!*" cried some of the children.

"*Yeeeeuuuuch!*" cried the rest.

"James!" cried the class teacher. "Your worms certainly are lively. I think you had better take them outside into the playground. Put them in the shade and come back inside. We don't want worms wiggling around the classroom."

At the sound of the commotion, Wilfred, Wayne and Wilhemina paused in mid-flight. They felt a bit silly clinging to the wooden sides, but there didn't seem to be anything to do but to stay completely still and sort of pretend they weren't there. James stood the wormery under a tree and ran back into school. Now that his worms had mixed up all the soil in the wormery, he was a bit fed up with them anyway. He didn't think it would matter very much if they *did* escape.

Escape? You should have seen the speed with which those worms were over the side and dropping safely down to the fresh, green grass beneath. They were a credit to Wilfred's training. Wilfred buried his head under the ground and put all his senses to use. There was something very familiar about the smell and taste of things around here.

"Follow me!" he cried, and off he wiggled at a speed that would have done him credit in the Worm Olympics.

In a remarkably short time, Wilfred found himself in familiar territory. When he saw a well-loved pink tail wiggling ahead of him, he didn't hesitate.

"Mum!" he yelled.

Mrs. Worm was overjoyed to see her son. She didn't comment on the fact that it was only twenty-four hours since he had left them. Time passes very slowly for worms.

"Wilfred!" she called. "Have you really been all around the world?"

"Almost," said Wilfred, who was a truthful worm at heart. "Just wait till I tell you what I've been doing."

Next time you are digging in your garden and find a little group of worms all wiggling together, do try not to disturb them. It's probably Wilfred telling the story of his adventures *again*. Leave them a couple of minutes and they'll *all* fall asleep—except Wilfred, of course. He'll be the wiggliest one of all.

The Lazy
Leopards

The other animals all agreed. Something would have to be done.

"What they do in their own time is up to them," said a lioness, "but when it's a case of cleaning up and teaching the little ones, they really should pull their weight. I've lost count of the number of carcasses I've fallen across this week."

"It was kind of you to call them to our attention," smiled the hyenas, licking their lips.

They were talking about the leopards, of course. Those leopards were incredibly lazy. They spent all day lolling about in trees, dozing or chatting. They behaved as if no one else existed and refused to play their part in the ordinary animal duties of everyday life.

"Someone is going to have to speak to them again," said an elephant. "I did it last time, so it can't be me. What about one of you giraffes?"

"Not likely," replied the senior giraffe, loftily. "I'm not going anywhere near them. Last week one of the youngsters had the audacity to stalk my ancient Aunt Agatha. The poor old girl was shaken out of her wits. She hasn't many of them as it is. I refuse to address another word to those loutish leopards."

The other animals shook their heads in horror.

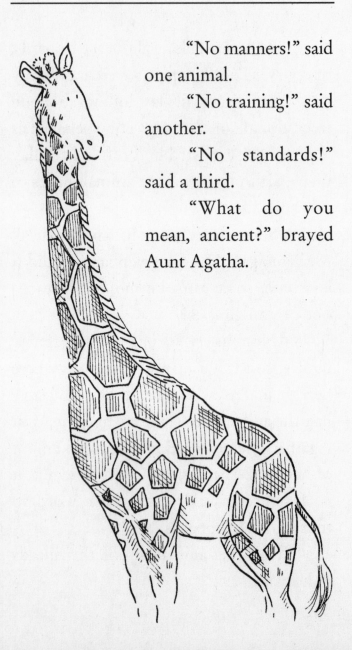

"No manners!" said one animal.

"No training!" said another.

"No standards!" said a third.

"What do you mean, ancient?" brayed Aunt Agatha.

"I suggest we all calm down and think sensibly about this," said a lion who was almost as ancient as Aunt Agatha, when the other animals had all finished tut-tutting and ho-humming.

"Naturally, we are anxious to hear what you have to say, O King," grovelled the hyenas.

"Now, now, none of that silly King nonsense," growled the lion. "You know we did away with all that years ago. But I have lived in this part of the savannah for a very long time and I'm sure, if I cast my mind back, I can think of other situations in which we have had to be pretty firm with some animal or other. Yes, now, I remember a time when the warthogs got a bit boisterous at the waterhole."

"It was a *very* long time ago," put in a warthog for the information of the younger animals present. These days, the warthogs were terribly proper and respectable members of the community.

"Quite, quite," said the lion in a soothing voice. "But I seem to remember that the action we took then was most effective. We simply didn't speak to the warthogs or acknowledge them in any way for a month or so. They were soon keen to be friends again. For one thing, if you'll forgive me saying so, warthog, they couldn't bear not hearing all the gossip."

"We like to keep informed, that is all," said the warthog stiffly. "And, with all due respect, sir, I don't think that would work in this case. I'm inclined to think that the leopards wouldn't even notice if one of us *did* speak to them. They'd notice even less if one of us didn't."

The other animals nodded their heads—all except the hyenas, who didn't like to appear to be disagreeing with the lion, so looked casually at the sky instead and rolled their eyes.

"I have another suggestion," said a young and rather aggressive elephant. The warthogs moved discreetly further from him. They remembered an unfortunate squashing incident the last time this same elephant got frisky in the waterhole.

"I suggest we stop talking and *do* something," said the elephant. "My idea would be to give their trees a brisk shaking. A few bruised leopard bottoms and we'd soon see a change of attitude. I'd be happy to carry out the mission myself."

But the old lion shook his head. "I don't think that will get us anywhere at all," he said. "Leopards are cats, after all. They're not going to land on their ... *ahem* ... bottoms. They will land on their feet, as cats do. And they'll just laugh, I think, which will be doubly annoying."

The other animals had to agree.

"How about food?" asked a plump little zebra who was always sorry to miss his supper. "If we could somehow stop them from catching anything to eat, they'd soon have to toe the line."

"Your instincts are good, young Stripy," said the lion, "but I'm afraid that your suggestion is not practical. We can't stop the leopards from catching food. They are faster than any of us. And if we persuaded the antelopes and gnus to move away, well, some of the rest of us would go hungry, too. Speaking personally, I don't fancy the idea."

There was a small silence.

"Maybe we just have to put up with them," said a vulture. "What does it matter if the odd carcass is left lying around? I think they can look quite attractive, myself, properly stripped, that is."

Another silence reigned for a long minute.

"Look," said the lion, "I think we all realize that we have slightly different ... er ... notions of how things should be. But we're going to have to work together on this. What you just said has given me an idea, vulture. Although I appreciate that the animals responsible for all this difficulty are the leopards, I wonder if we shouldn't just face the fact that they are never, never, *ever* going to do their duty. In that case, we either have to put up with things the way they are, or we have to do something about it ourselves."

"You're right," agreed the lioness. "We could talk all day and still not have any effect on the way those lazy leopards behave. Why, look at them just now. What are they doing? What they do every day. They're just lying about in trees until they feel hungry. And meanwhile, all their youngsters either doze with the grown-ups or run around making nuisances of themselves here on the savannah. They are totally undisciplined and full of mischief. If they were not so fast on their feet, they'd never catch anything. You should just hear them crashing about through the long grass. They sound like a herd of great elephants out hunting. Sorry, elephant."

"No offence taken," trumpeted the elephant. "I do understand what you mean. We, of course, do not hunt, so it doesn't matter if we 'crash about', as you put it. But it's distressing to see a young animal attempting to hunt with so little finesse. In my young day…"

The other animals all started talking quickly. Once the elephant got going on his young day, it could be weeks before he stopped. Elephants, as you know, never forget anything, but it is really *not* very interesting to hear (again!) what they had for breakfast on a Tuesday morning seven years ago.

At last, the lion called the meeting to order.

"Here's my suggestion," he said. "The hyenas and the vultures are in charge of carcass-disposal. I'm sure they'll make a good job of it."

"No problem," said the hyenas with wide grins.

"What about the bones?" asked the vultures. "We can't crunch the great big ones, you know."

"A tidy pile in that little grove of trees over there will be fine," said the lion. "And please ask the elephants if you have difficulty in lifting anything."

"Any job undertaken, no matter how large or small," said the old elephant.

A warthog had another query.

"What about the carcasses those leopards pull up into the trees with them?" she asked. "We're not asking the hyenas to go up there, are we?"

"Climbing isn't our strong point," said one hyena.

"Going too close to leopards isn't big on our list of ambitions either," said another, "much as we would like to help."

"I think," said the lion, "that we can only deal with carcasses the leopards have finished with. We must leave their strange practices in trees to them. Now, about the youngsters…"

"Yes, what are we going to do about them?" asked Aunt Agatha with interest.

"In a word, training," said the lion, impressively. "And that means, I think, those of us who hunt. Which means…"

"Which means it's a job for lions," said the lioness briskly. "I think you'd better leave it to the ladies, sir, if you don't mind. We have more experience of this sort of thing and we're used to training our cubs, as well."

"That would be excellent," said the lion. "I'd suggest a programme of first-level stalking, the elementary spring, killing for beginners, and some dragging practice. What do you think?"

"We'll work out a programme and let you approve it," smiled the lioness diplomatically. She knew perfectly well that the lion's knowledge of hunting was purely theoretical, whereas she had stalked and killed more antelopes than he had had warm dinners—actually, she had stalked and killed exactly as many antelopes as he had had warm dinners.

The vultures were looking a little restless, hopping from foot to foot and flapping their wings, which always made the other animals jumpy.

"Yes?" said the lion wearily. He sometimes felt that there had been less work to do when he *was* King of the Savannah. Then, his word was law. Now, there was a lot of talking before *anything* got done.

"We're very happy to help, of course," said the head vulture, "but I always think that *fairness* is important. No one wants to feel *put upon*. We all need to *work together*." At each heavily emphasized word, he flapped his wings even harder.

The lion shook his head.

"What is he talking about?" he asked the lioness.

"I think," she purred softly, "that he is becoming a little anxious that not *all* the animals are contributing. The hyenas, the vultures and the lions, yes. But what about the others?"

Several of the other animals caught the end of her speech.

"I'd like to offer lessons in tooth-care and dental hygiene," said a warthog. "We have to take great care of our tusks, and I think I can say I'm an expert."

"Excellent," said the lion. "Now, what about you zebras?"

The zebras looked at each other in alarm. None of them wanted to offer to help the leopards learn to hunt, for obvious reasons. Anyway, the zebras only knew about hunting from a *hunted* point of view. They didn't feel they had much to offer.

"Could I make a suggestion?" asked the lioness, feeling that she really should have had a career in the diplomatic corps. "What about general policing duties? The zebras are fast on their feet and can gallop about all over the savannah. They could report on any carcasses left lying around (muttering from the vultures and squeaks of wounded pride from the hyenas) and keep a look-out for any young leopards up to no good."

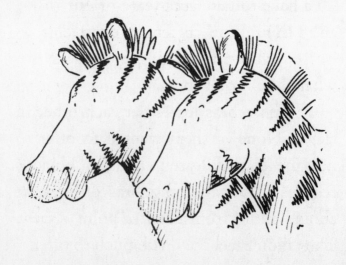

The zebras looked pleased. This sounded just right for them and kept them well out of the way when leopards were doing prowling practice.

"That only leaves us," commented Aunt Agatha. "What about if we watched the leopards in their trees? Discreetly, of course. We're on a level with them and can see if they're up to anything unpleasant."

"I think that loud snoring is as unpleasant as it gets," said the lion, "but it's a good idea. Thank you, giraffe."

There were a few more details to wrap up, but the meeting was essentially over. Besides, the lioness was beginning to feel hungry, and the zebra, who knew the signs, was anxious to be off.

"We'll start tomorrow," said the old lion. "And we'll meet again here in ... let's see ... exactly a week's time to discuss progress. How about that?"

The next seven days were busy ones for the animals of the savannah. The hyenas and the vultures grew fat and happy dealing with carcass-disposal. They were less keen on piling up the bones, but when the old lion insisted, they cleared those up as well.

The lionesses found that they rather enjoyed having young cubs to boss around without the heavy responsibility of parenthood. And leopards made very good pupils. In particular, their creeping and pouncing skills developed, as it were, by leaps and bounds.

Everyone got a bit tired of the zebras, who galloped around the whole time, making it their business to find out what *everyone* was doing, but they meant well and at least didn't spend the whole time moaning as they usually did.

As for the warthogs' lessons in tooth-care and dental hygiene, they were a triumph! In fact, several of the animals joined the young leopards in their lessons, having never fully come to grips with the subject themselves. Even Aunt Agatha, casually chomping on a nearby tree and pretending not to listen, picked up a tip or two for her worn old gnashers.

With everyone so busy, there was surprisingly little grumbling on the wide savannah. Everyone felt useful and happy. Only one group of animals was excluded.

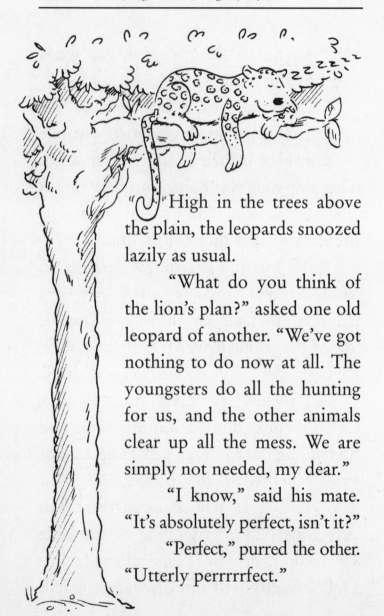

"High in the trees above the plain, the leopards snoozed lazily as usual.

"What do you think of the lion's plan?" asked one old leopard of another. "We've got nothing to do now at all. The youngsters do all the hunting for us, and the other animals clear up all the mess. We are simply not needed, my dear."

"I know," said his mate. "It's absolutely perfect, isn't it?"

"Perfect," purred the other. "Utterly perrrrfect."

The Perfect Polar Bear

If you ask anyone what colour a polar bear is, he or she will reply without the slightest hesitation.

"Is this some kind of trick? They're white, of course!"

Everyone knows that snow is white, and that the fur of polar bears helps to camouflage them in the snowy wastes of the Arctic Circle. So polar bears must be white. Right?

Wrong! If you have ever seen a polar bear, you will know that it wouldn't win any washing-powder whiteness prizes. Its fur is a kind of dirty, creamy, yellowy colour. Those pristine white fluffy bears you can buy for babies are way off the mark. Polar bears are shaggy and grubby, and no kind of advertizement for the purity of the icy world of the North Pole.

If you think about it, it stands to reason. How do polar bears keep clean in the Arctic? Do they jump under a hot shower when their fur gets grubby? Do they toddle down to the Polar Bear Beauty Parlour when they want to go just a little bit blonder? No, of course not. The only place they have for a good wash is the Atlantic Ocean. It's not a brilliant turquoise like the Caribbean. It's not a shimmering blue like the Mediterranean.

It's grey. And not a very clean-looking grey at that.

You can't really blame the sea, either. How can a piece of water that's packed with fish, and seals, and the oily hulls of fishing boats possibly keep clean? I don't like to mention it, but every one of those swimmers and floaters is using the sea for *all* its biological functions. Know what I mean? Let's not talk any more about it. It will put you off your fishfingers.

So, as I say, it's no one's fault, really, that polar bears are not white. You can't blame those bears at all. I'm sure they do their best to keep clean in very difficult conditions. And, come to think of it, you don't often hear of Arctic explorers taking baths either, do you? In fact, the North

Pole is a good deal smellier and dirtier than you might think.

Polar bears, I'm happy to say, are unaware of any lack of personal hygiene among their friends and relations. And you can be sure that none of the smaller animals is going to say a word. They all live in fear of polar bears, who are bigger, stronger, faster and fiercer than anyone else on the ice. The only living creatures that polar bears have to worry about are humans, and most of them would rather sit at home in warm sitting rooms, watching polar bears on television, than venture into the freezing wastes of Greenland and all points north. Which is just as well for the polar bears.

This story concerns a polar bear family with a difference. Pellida and Paolo Polar Bear got together one long dark winter and found that they had a lot in common—ice, fur, black noses, and a love of fresh cod (uncooked and preferably in large quantities). With so many shared interests, it wasn't surprising that they soon decided to make things permanent. Not long after that, they decided to start a family of their own.

Pellida dug herself a beautiful ice-cave and settled down to await the arrival of her cubs. Paolo was most attentive, bringing little treats of fish-heads and seal-livers whenever she was peckish. It doesn't sound attractive to us, but these are the red roses and champagne of the polar bear world. Pellida looked smug and Paolo was proud and happy.

He was even prouder and happier the day that Pellida produced two fine cubs. The pleased parents decided to call the little girl Pearl and the boy Pedro. They were very cute, fluffy, cuddly cubs, soon surrounded by adoring aunts and uncles with lots of useless advice on the raising of fine, upstanding bears.

Later, much later, Pellida and Paolo wondered if they had made a mistake in naming their daughter Pearl. After all, a pearl is a lustrous, white, gleaming jewel. A polar bear, an ordinary polar bear, is a shaggy, hairy, creamy, yellowish animal.

But they were not to know what was going to happen.

Polar bear cubs are, of course, not as shaggy, hairy, creamy or yellowish as their parents. Their fur is fluffy and clean. You still couldn't really say it is white, not in the way that white bathtubs and white toothpastes are white, but they are a lot whiter than their parents. Pearl was still very, very young when she realized this, and she felt pretty pleased to be so clean and pretty compared with her mother.

At this stage, the cubs were still in their ice-cave. The cave, after being lived in for several months and suffering as the scene of several fish-head suppers, was not very gleaming and pristine either. That is why, the first time that Pearl found out what whiteness really is like was the first time her mother led her out of the cave into the fresh, sparkling snow and ice outside. Pearl simply couldn't believe it.

"Mummy, Mummy, help!" she cried, as her brother ran off to play in the snow. "I'm all dirty, look!"

Pellida looked, but all she could see was a perfectly normal polar bear cub standing in some perfectly normal snow.

"No, you're not," she said. "You look fine. What's the matter?"

But Pearl was genuinely distressed. "Look!" she cried again. And she showed Pellida her little fluffy paw against the whiteness of the snow. Certainly, the cold stuff was a lot whiter than Pearl's little paw, but Pellida still couldn't see what the problem was. It took a long time for Pearl, who hadn't been taught how to talk about colours in the cave, to explain what she was worried about.

Pellida looked perplexed. She really couldn't see what all the fuss was about, but if the little one really felt she wasn't clean, then a dip in the ocean was the answer to all her problems.

"Come along," said Pellida. "You'll soon be clean. It's time you both learnt to swim, anyway." And she led the way to the edge of the ice, where the waters of the Atlantic Ocean slapped and slopped against the towering sides of icebergs.

"You'll both be excellent swimmers," said Pellida. "All you have to do is jump in. Look, I'll show you!"

With an almighty splash, Pellida plopped into the water. There was plenty of time, she thought, to show her cubs the finer points of diving.

Pedro hesitated for a moment. Then he ran towards the edge on his little furry feet. Just before he got there, he changed his mind and slammed on the brakes, but it was too late. His four paws settled into a skid and shot him inexorably towards the water. His splash was much smaller than his mother's, but the result was the same. In another moment he was bobbing around happily in the water and waving to his sister.

"Come on in, Pearl!" he called. "It's lovely! And it's not cold at all!"

Pearl stood aghast on the ice.

"You must be joking!" she shuddered. "I'm not coming into that filthy water. It's even greyer and dingier than I am! There's no way I'm ever going in."

Pellida frowned. A polar bear who can't swim is a polar bear who can't eat. You can wait for a long time for a seal to be silly enough to haul itself up on the ice and sit there looking like dinner.

Paolo had been watching from the shore and saw Pellida's distress.

"Don't worry," he said. "She'll get used to it. I'll take her for a brisk roll in the snow instead. You have a long swim with Pedro. And if you happen to come across some fat cod while you're there…"

Pearl was happy to roll in the snow, but after that all she wanted to do was to sit down and lick her claws clean. In the end, Paolo made sure she was in a safe place and went off to check on the cod-catching situation.

The polar bear parents were hopeful that Pearl's problem with the ocean would pass, but it didn't. In time, Pedro became a very fine cod-catcher. He could dive, swim and glide underwater with grace and speed. He tried hard to persuade his sister that it was fun.

"On land," he said, "we're sort of big and lumbering. But underwater, we're as speedy as fish. You'd really like it."

Pearl shook her head. "You speak for yourself," she said. "*I* don't lumber on land. And I have *never* wanted to be at all like a fish. They're smelly!"

Pearl's view of the ocean didn't change—until the day that she and her mother frightened away a fisherman sitting patiently beside a hole in the ice. Pearl peered down into the hole and was just about to turn away in disgust at the sight of a pool full of grey water when ... she noticed that it was full of her! Unlike the restless water on the coast, the water in the hole was almost still, and Pearl could see a beautiful reflection of herself peering back at her. She thought she looked pretty good. No matter what her mother said, Pearl refused to move on. She stared in fascination at her reflection, turning her face in a vain attempt to see what the back of her head looked like. She was terribly disappointed when, a few hours later, the hole iced over.

It wasn't long before Pearl's attitude caused serious problems in the polar bear family. It wasn't that she was lazy. She was quite happy to help dig ice-caves, as long as the ice wasn't so hard it scratched her claws. But Pearl simply refused to go fishing. At first, Pedro was proud to bring the fish he had caught to his sister. She had just as big an appetite as he had. But after a while he began to feel that it was unfair.

"She doesn't catch them. Why should she eat them?" he asked his father.

Paolo wrinkled his nose. "You have a point, my son," he said, "but what's the alternative? We can't let your sister starve."

"Why not?" asked Pedro coldly. "Anyway, I don't think she would. I think she'd start swimming straight away once she got hungry."

Paolo talked the matter over with Pellida that evening.

"He could be right," he said. "We could give it a try."

Pellida was reluctant to see her daughter suffer, but she agreed. Looking to the future, she was afraid that a polar bear who couldn't fish would never find a husband and raise a family of her own.

The next morning, Pellida explained to Pearl that she would have to do her own fishing from now on.

Pearl simply didn't understand. "But I can't," she said.

"Then you will have to go hungry," replied Pellida, hardening her heart.

After that, Paolo, Pellida and Pedro ate their meals in the water.

Pearl watched from the ice for a while. Her tummy began to rumble. She peered down into the grey water. Could she? No! Would she? No! She turned on her heel and walked away across the ice and snow with as much dignity as she could muster. She already felt a little faint from lack of fish but she had had an idea.

Over the next few days, Pellida kept a close eye on her daughter whenever she was herself out of the water. A polar bear can only last so long without food. But Pearl showed no signs of flagging. He coat was as thick and her eyes were as bright as ever. In fact, if anything, Pearl was looking a little happier than usual. It was strange.

Days passed. Weeks passed. Pearl went from strength to strength. She was growing up now, and some of the young male bears were beginning to follow her around with silly smiles on their faces.

"I believe I've solved the mystery," Pellida told Paolo. "That young minx is probably getting her admirers to fish for her. No wonder she isn't getting thinner."

But Paolo shook his head. "Male bears are taught from an early age," he said, "that the first thing you should look for in a wife is good fishing skills. I've had words with Pedro about it myself. A black nose and shining eyes are no use at all if a lady bear can't fish. Take it from me, those bears are not fishing for Pearl. I've had a horrible thought, though. What if she is *stealing* fish from other bears?"

Pellida was horrified. She didn't want to think that her daughter was a thief. Two minutes' thought made her feel a little calmer.

"That's silly," she said. "Where would she be stealing fish *from*? All the other polar bears are like us. They eat their fish fresh, as soon as they have caught them. They don't leave them lying about for another bear to steal. No, there is only one explanation. She must just be too proud to let us know that we were right. She has to be waiting until we are

asleep and then slipping into the water by herself and doing her own fishing then."

"Well, there's only one way to find out," said Paolo. "We'll have to watch her and see what she does."

Polar bears are not really built for undercover surveillance. Paolo's attempts to pretend to be an iceberg when watching his daughter were pretty pathetic. But there really isn't anything else you can pretend to be in the Arctic. Paolo's seal-impressions were impossibly bad.

Paolo's ability to stay awake was impossibly bad, too. After three nights when he had to confess to Pellida that he had failed to watch his daughter for more than an hour or two, Pellida decided to join him. Frankly, two large polar bears pretending to be icebergs are no more convincing than one, but at least Pellida was able to nudge Paolo each time he started to snore.

The anxious parents waited for what seemed like hours. Pearl simply did what all self-respecting polar bears were doing at that time. She slept. Paolo slept too, in between nudges. Pellida got fed up.

"I'm hungry!" she hissed to Paolo. "Let's go and get some breakfast!"

"Good idea!" whispered Paolo with relief. "I couldn't sit here a moment longer. I don't know how those icebergs stand it."

For a polar bear capable of making such a very silly remark, Paolo's next thought was remarkably sensible.

"Me meen mimiots!" he shouted, bobbing to the surface with a fish in his mouth. When he had swallowed the fish, he made more sense.

"We've been idiots! This is when she does her fishing—while we are! She must just do it somewhere else. If we creep back on to the ice, we'll catch her coming back and get an idea of the general direction," he said.

Back on shore, Pellida and Paolo trotted to the top of an ice hill to look around. When they spotted Pearl, they could hardly believe their eyes. She *was* fishing, but she wasn't getting her fur wet. She was using the line left behind by the fleeing angler to fish through a hole in the ice—and admire her own reflection at the same time. She was oblivious to the young male bears who sat admiringly at a respectful distance.

Pellida and Paolo sighed.

"Who says beauty and brains don't go together?" asked Pellida.

"That's my girl," grinned Paolo.

Tortoise
Trouble

I'm sure you must know the story of the tortoise and the hare. They have a race and, because the hare is over-confident, the tortoise wins. What you may not know is that tortoises have been living on the glory of this for years. Frankly, it has made them unpleasantly uppity.

Hares, on the other hand, have felt embarrassed about the whole thing for just as long. When you're a creature renowned for its speed, it's annoying to be reminded all the time about a solitary unfortunate incident centuries ago. Since then, hares have done their best to improve their reputations. They train on a regular basis, whatever the weather. They are faster now than they have ever been, beating their own world records each year. They also try not to be boastful, lazy or stupid. On the first two points, they are doing pretty well. In fact, you won't find

a more modest or hardworking bunch of animals anywhere. But hares never have been the Einsteins of the animal kingdom, as this story will show.

These days, hares and tortoises tend to keep well clear of each other. Tortoises have been known to claim that hares have a vicious streak and are always looking for revenge. In fact, tortoises are simply scared out of their wits that an enterprising hare will demand a rematch. Sadly, hares are about as enterprising as they are bright, so this has never occurred to them.

They keep out of the way of tortoises simply because they can't stand to be reminded of their day of shame.

There was a time when tortoises were quite often kept as pets by human beings. Since tortoises can live for a very, very long time, some of them still are. The tortoise in this story was called Speedy. It was a joke made by Speedy's first owner, but the tortoise took it very seriously. He'd heard the tortoise-and-hare story, you see.

Speedy spent his summers strolling about the garden, munching the leaves and fruit that his owner put out for him. He spent his winters sleeping peacefully in a box of straw in the owner's garage. This went on for years and years and years, until the owner grew up and went away to college. The same winter, the owner's parents decided to move home, now that there were only two of them in the house. It was a very hard winter. What with the problems of the removal van getting stuck in the snow and the removal men slipping over on the ice, no one thought about Speedy in the garage. The removal men saw what they thought was a box full of straw and left it.

Five hundred miles away, in their new home, the owner's parents found their lives filled with removing some truly revolting carpets and repairing some very dodgy plumbing. They didn't give a thought to a sleeping tortoise. Back at their old house, the new owners were abroad for a year. They employed a man to look around the place once a week, keep the garden tidy and make sure there had been no break-ins. They didn't dream there was already someone in residence who might need to break out rather than in.

One sunny day in early spring, Speedy opened his eyes and felt a little peckish. It was time, he decided, that someone came to let him out of his box. But no one came. Speedy waited for a week or two. His peckishness gradually grew, until his shell felt too big for him and he discovered himself to be distinctly hungry. If no one was coming to open the box, Speedy decided it was time to do it for himself.

Luckily, this proved to be pretty easy. The box was lying on its side and it wasn't fastened. All Speedy had to do was to push open the flaps with his nose and venture outside. He found, of course, that he was in the garage. There's nothing wrong with garages as a general rule, but for a hungry tortoise they are distinctly lacking in any form of nourishment. Speedy tried the big, metal doors and found they made an interesting clanging sound when he charged at them with his head. But they didn't open.

Next, Speedy tried the wooden side door. This made a deep booming noise when he charged at it. But it didn't open either. Then Speedy noticed that there was a little door within the door. It had been used by a stray cat that the family once looked after. She was always too scared to come into the house, but she liked to sit on the bonnet of the car in cold weather.

It goes without saying that cat-flaps were not designed for tortoises. Their legs are too short, for one thing. Speedy was getting hungrier by the minute, however, and in such situations his brain was pretty agile. He pushed a pile of old newspapers under the cat-flap, climbed up on them, and succeeded at last in pushing the little door open. Of course, there were no newspapers on the other side, so Speedy's descent was a little less elegant, but he *had* escaped from the garage.

Speedy's mind was now on only one thing. Food! He set off down the garden at a surprising speed (but not fast enough to beat a hare in normal circumstances) in search of something tasty to eat.

Now the garden had been well stocked and well tended, but it was a modern garden with very little of interest to a hungry tortoise. Bamboos, cacti and small trees are of very little use to a short-legged animal longing for a lettuce leaf. Nevertheless, Speedy did nibble at most of the things he could reach. They all tasted disgusting and left an unpleasantly queasy feeling in his tummy.

Speedy was just beginning to feel desperate when he reached the end of the garden. Behind a hedge (not edible—Speedy did try) was a wire-netting fence. Beyond the fence was a sight to gladden any tortoise's eye. It was a field of big, green cabbages.

I don't suppose you have ever seen a tortoise climbing over a wire-netting fence. Let's just say that in an Olympic event of such an activity, he would have scored less than nothing for Style and Artistic Interpretation but quite a lot for Difficulty. A tortoise fired by the sight of several thousand cabbages, however, can achieve great things. Several hours later, Speedy fell with a thud on to a particularly huge cabbage and proceeded to start munching through it before he had even got his breath back. Nothing had ever tasted so good.

For the next few days, Speedy's life took on a regular pattern. He woke up in the morning and started munching. He had a little doze during the warmest part of the day. He munched his way through the afternoon and then called it a day. It was a simple life, but after several months in a cardboard box, even simple things seem exciting to a tortoise.

Speedy's life might have gone on in this way for weeks if he hadn't had his fateful meeting with the hare. He was munching his way through a cabbage one morning—nothing strange in that—when he suddenly became aware that someone else was munching from the other side. Another couple of munches and he all of a sudden found himself nose-to-nose with a long-eared furry animal.

"Aaaagh!" cried Speedy.

"Aaaagh!" cried the hare.

It was only after his initial fright that Speedy realized he was looking at a hare. He had never seen one in the flesh before, but he had heard so much about those long ears and longer legs. The hare had never seen a tortoise before, either, but there are not many animals with short legs and a hard shell. Gradually, the expressions on the faces of both animals changed to one of deep suspicion.

"What are you doing here?" asked the hare.

"I might ask you the same question," said Speedy loftily.

"I suppose you want to race," said the hare, showing several centuries of hare *v.* tortoise paranoia.

"Naturally," said Speedy, showing centuries of a totally unwarranted sense of superiority. "I'm ready when you are. Prepare to be humiliated—again."

Now Speedy knew perfectly well that he didn't stand a chance of beating the hare, but he was carried away by the drama of the moment. He also had an obscure hope that the race might not actually happen. After all, you couldn't race in a field full of cabbages. In the meantime, he felt that a show of confidence was the best way of standing up for tortoise-kind.

The hare also knew perfectly well that he should win. He looked down at Speedy's little legs and heavy shell and could tell at once that on paper there was no contest. He himself was young and fit. He was even faster than most of the hares he knew. Surely he could beat a tortoise in his sleep? But hares, as you know, are not very clever. Speedy's confidence was pretty alarming. Was there something that the tortoise knew but the hare didn't? It crossed the hare's mind, and it was a very horrible thought, that maybe tortoises could do some kind of hypnotism. Rabbits, he knew, were prone to being mesmerized by the headlights of cars. Could it be that hares were susceptible to the beady eyes of tortoises? The hare tried not to look at Speedy. The shifty look this gave him made the tortoise even more confident.

(I should perhaps mention at this point that by a strange twist of fate, the hare's name was also Speedy. This time it wasn't a joke. But since it would be much, much too confusing for both characters in this story to have the same name, I'll just call him "the hare".)

Back in the cabbage field, Speedy was just beginning to hope that the subject had been forgotten about when the hare said, "We can't race here, among all these cabbages. There's a grassy meadow over there. Let's go."

Off shot the hare at frightening (to a tortoise) speed. He was out of sight before Speedy had got his first foot into gear. The tortoise realized with some relief that it was going to take him several days to cross the vast cabbage field and reach the meadow. Maybe on the way he could think of a plan.

We needn't go into detail about the next few days. Suffice it to say that Speedy plodded slowly on and every so often the hare came running back to make sure he was still coming. Naturally, during this process the hare began to get some of his confidence back. It did seem to him that a tortoise who couldn't travel at speed over a cabbage field would not be too nippy over grass.

At long last, Speedy reached the fence that separated the meadow from the cabbages. It wasn't, as Speedy had hoped, something that would be very difficult for him to climb over, it was an electric fence with a big gap at the bottom. He crawled through with ease. The hare, however, whose nerves were beginning to show again, forgot to lower his ears and got a toe-tingling shock.

As the hare attempted to recover his composure, Speedy surveyed the meadow. It was neither empty nor flat. Its steep slope was being nibbled by about twenty woolly, bleating sheep, who looked up with interest at the newcomers. One sheep came over to investigate. The others came too. They had rarely seen a hare sitting still and had never seen a tortoise at all. It was the highlight of their year.

For forty minutes, the hare and the tortoise tried to explain to the sheep about the historic race and today's rematch. It was uphill work. Sheep make hares seem positively bursting with intelligence. At last the racers gave up. They asked the sheep to stand to one side and begged one of them to be the starter. It took several further minutes of intensive training for the selected sheep to grasp that she had to say, "Ready, steady, *baa*!" at just the right moment. Making her understand when the right moment was took another few minutes. By the time the sheep were ready and the hare and the tortoise had done some limbering-up exercises, it was late in the afternoon. The sun was starting to set.

As they lined up at the start, both the hare and the tortoise realized there was a problem, but neither liked to be the first to say so. Luckily, the starter-sheep spoke up instead.

"Baa! This is no good!" she said. "The sun is in my eyes."

The solution was simple. They would run *down* the meadow instead of *up* the meadow. The spectator-sheep would stay where they were to mark the finish line, the starter-sheep and the hare and the tortoise would trot up to the other end of the meadow to the new start line.

The poor tortoise found even walking up the steep meadow exhausting. The hare and the sheep waited impatiently at the top as he crawled to meet them. The hare, who had been eager and ready for the off a few minutes before, now found himself almost paralysed with nerves. He had to do a lot of deep breathing to calm himself.

At last the runners were ready. The starter-sheep was ready. Far below, the spectator-sheep were ready.

"Ready, steady, *baa*!" bleated the starter-sheep. And they were off! If only the slope hadn't been so steep!

Taking an early lead, as expected, the hare was dimly aware of gasps from the sheep below and something small and round flying past him. Unable to keep his footing on the steep slope, the tortoise had begun to roll. By instinct, he tucked in his head and feet and tail, making himself smooth and round. He shot down the slope at an incredible speed.

There was no hope for the hare. As he skidded to a stop at the bottom of the hill, the sheep were already clustered around a dazed tortoise and congratulating him with a deafening din of bleating.

So that is why the utterly unbearable uppitiness of tortoises and the shame of the humiliated hares continues to this day. Unless you have heard of another rematch somewhere?

Dinosaur
Doom

Once upon a time, there was a dinosaur who could predict the future. You might think that this was a useful skill. Surely a dinosaur might like to know when the next Tyrannosaurus was going to come crashing through the undergrowth? And forewarning of the odd Ice Age could be useful, too. Alas, as is so often the way with clairvoyants of all species, no one believed a word that Derek (that was his name) said.

Derek himself was a medium-sized dinosaur who was as happy to snack on an early mammal or a plate of eggs as he was to munch a large leaf. Many of his friends were less omnivorous. The herbivores, who ate only plants, should have listened much more carefully to what Derek told them. An incident that happened one sunny spring morning is typical.

Derek was strolling through the forest with his friend Herbert. A large, slow plant-eater, Herbert had to make frequent stops to nibble at the ferns and palms through which they were swishing.

"I don't know how you can bear to eat those little creeping things, Derek," he mumbled, with his mouth half full of leaves. "I couldn't bear the idea of having to crunch through all those horrible little bones. And as for getting the fur stuck in your teeth. Yeeeeuuuch!"

"You get used to it," said Derek calmly. "Haven't you finished with that fern yet, Herbert? We'll never get to the lake today at this rate. I was hoping for a little fish or shellfish for my supper."

"I wouldn't mind trying a bit of waterweed, too," agreed Herbert, taking one last mouthful. "All right then, let's get going again."

On they went, with Derek skipping along beside Herbert, constantly annoyed by his slow plodding.

"Herbert," he complained, "can't you walk *any* faster? If I was as slow as you, I'd *have* to be a vegetarian. I'd never be able to catch anything that moved."

(Some interesting questions of the "Which came first, the chicken or the egg?" variety are raised by Derek's words, but this story is not the place to consider them. We will pass swiftly on—which is

more than lumbering Herbert was capable
of doing.)

Much, much later, the friends
reached the lake and spent a pleasant and
lazy afternoon snacking on the various
edible plants and creatures that lived
there. At last it was time to come home.

The sun was beginning to set as the
friends went back into the forest once
more, and right away Derek had that
funny feeling in his spine that often meant
something not-quite-pleasant was going
to happen.

"Herbert," he said, "let's walk a little more quickly. I've got a strange sense of something being not quite right. It's as if someone is watching us."

Herbert had a good look around.

"I can't see anyone," he said. "My eyes aren't as sharp as yours, of course, but even so, I think you're worrying about nothing. Anyway, I can't walk any faster. My tummy is full of waterweed and I'm not sure it quite likes it. I've got a sort of swimmy, swooshy feeling in the place where I like to feel full. I might even need to stop for a while."

"No! Please, *please*, Herbert, don't stop!" begged Derek. "I can't begin to explain what a bad idea that would be. A swimmy, swooshy feeling would be the least of your problems, believe me. Come *on*! We've got to hurry!" And Derek even tried to push his friend along the path.

Of course, Derek was right to feel alarmed. Only a couple of minutes later, there was a terrifying roaring and raging from the bushes. Out leapt an Allosaurus, hungry and hostile. He took one look at Derek's sinewy form and pushed him aside. Big, fat Herbert looked much more like a healthy first course.

Derek did his best, but he was no match for the vicious attacker. Within seconds, Derek was injured and Herbert was dinner. Before Derek's horrified eyes, the Allosaurus made short work of the meal that had been Herbert. Only a few hefty bones were left.

Luckily for Derek, the Allosaurus couldn't eat another mouthful when he had finished. As he snoozed under a tree, Derek limped back home.

Back in the Dinosaur Den, where Derek and his friends met most Saturday nights, Derek's friends listened to his story without much sympathy.

"Pull the other one, Derek," they hooted. "It's the same with all your spooky stories. There's never any *proof*! If you'd brought Herbert to back you up, that would be another thing. Then we might believe you."

Derek was dancing up and down with frustration.

"But that's just the point," he cried. "If Herbert was alive and well I wouldn't be telling this story! I can't prove it when Herbert is history and the Allosaurus is fast asleep under a tree somewhere.

Should I go and find him and bring him back here? Is that what you want?"

"Now, now, none of that talk here," said the landlord. "You're lucky we let you in, Derek, though I wouldn't let my little ones anywhere near you. You know we don't let carnivores in here as a general rule. And that goes double for those Allosauruses. They're the worst of the bunch. Why, my Aunt Mildred..."

"...and my friend Herbert..." said Derek, but he muttered it under his breath. He knew that no one believed in his second sight. He went off to sit by himself in a corner and think a few sad thoughts about poor Herbert. Somehow, he felt responsible, although he was no match for an Allosaurus.

What happened to Herbert was particularly painful for Derek (and not only because the Allosaurus gave him a nasty nip on the knee), but it was by no means unusual. Time and again Derek tried to warn his friends about something that was going to happen. Time and again they ignored him. One day, his friend Godfrey took him on one side.

"It's like this, Derek," he said, "you're not making it any easier for yourself. Whether you can see into the future or not, I couldn't say, but no one wants to hear bad news all the time. And that's all they ever hear from you. As soon as they see you coming, dinosaurs feel depressed. They know that you're about to tell them their grandfather will be attacked by a Velociraptor, or their children will be crushed by an Ultrasaurus. Even if it's true, and there's quite a lot of doubt about that, it isn't encouraging. And what makes you think they can *do* anything about it? If it's going to happen, it's going to happen. What's the point of knowing?"

(Hmm. Several very interesting philosophical points are raised by young Godfrey's speech, but once again, we must pass on. You can think about them when this story is over.)

Derek reflected on Godfrey's words. He didn't know whether telling people did any good or not, he simply felt that it was unfair to a friend to know that a tree was about to fall on his head and not to tell him. It's the kind of thing where afterwards the friend might say, "Why on earth didn't you tell me a tree was about to fall on my head?" Only, of course, *after* the tree fell, the friend wasn't there to complain. It was all a bit confusing.

After some more thought, Derek decided that he would try not always to be the bringer of bad news. After all, he could see all kinds of things in the future, and some of them were very jolly indeed.

"Hello, Humphrey!" he greeted the landlord one evening. "Congratulations on the triplets! Three babies at a time is very, very rare for your species! You and Juanita must be proud."

"Not yet," said Humphrey drily. "The eggs aren't due to hatch for a couple of weeks. So you think you know there are triplets? Are they boys or girls?"

"All girls," smiled Derek.

Humphrey tried to put Derek's words out of his mind and he very nearly succeeded. But a fortnight later, when the doctor called him into the hatching room and congratulated him on his three fine daughters, Humphrey couldn't help but feel a little disappointed. He should have been feeling on top of the world. Instead, he had the sense that someone had told him what was in his birthday presents before he opened them.

Poor Derek couldn't win. If he gave dinosaurs bad news, they didn't want to hear it. If he gave them good news, they didn't want to hear that either. He gave up trying to help his friends and settled down to concentrate on the numbers for each week's dinolottery. A month later, he retired to the slopes of Mount Mellifluous to live a life of ease.

Derek was not a cynical dinosaur, but he was a little surprised at how many friends he found he had once he came into money. They seemed delighted to visit him in his mansion, splash about in his Baryonyx-free swimming pool, and play Hurl-the-Rock on his magnificent full-sized court. Even those of his friends who had avoided his pronouncements before, now showed a flattering interest in his predictions.

"What's the weather going to be like tomorrow, Derek?" they would ask. "You're so very clever about that sort of thing."

"Any chance of telling us what next week's numbers for the dinolottery are, Derek?" others would ask him (only half-jokingly.) "We could move in next door."

As a matter of fact, most of them didn't need to move in next door as they had already moved in with Derek. His dozens of guest-rooms were full to over-flowing and his bills were mounting. Derek felt a sense of foreboding.

Yes, day by day, Derek became more and more sure that something truly dreadful was going to happen. Something so dreadful that his mind wouldn't even understand it properly. What could it be?

At first Derek assumed that he was going to lose all his dinoloot and be back where he started. But whenever he needed some more cash, he only had to win the dinolottery again, and that wasn't difficult. It was true that he had to do it under a different name each time, and once he had to disguise himself as an Oviraptor to pick up his prize, but none of these problems was difficult to solve. No, the dark, dark, impending doom was something different and much, much worse.

Derek next thought that Mount Mellifluous might be about to erupt. Little plumes of smoke were occasionally to be seen coming from the summit, and the water in the swimming pool grew warmer every day, fed by underground springs. But when he climbed to the top to see if his feelings grew any stronger, he found they didn't. Back under the palm trees, Derek tried to push the ever-worsening feeling to the back of his mind.

As Derek's mood got blacker, his guests began to wonder if the free food, drink and leisure activities were really worth the sight of their host's mournful face each morning.

"I wouldn't mind," said Humphrey, voicing the thoughts of many of those present, "but we all know *why* he's looking so miserable. He's had one of his premo… premowhatsits and he can't bring himself to tell us what it is. It's true that he's had some lucky guesses in the past, but none of us actually believes that he can see into the future. Why don't we let him tell us whatever it is, so that he feels better?"

There was some muttering at this. It was all very well for Humphrey, but if Derek foresaw a dreadful doom for one of the others, they couldn't help feeling it might spoil their afternoon. Perhaps even their week. On the other hand, Derek really was becoming painful to be near. It was like living with a big, black cloud in the vicinity.

To be fair, it was very much like that for Derek, too. But his situation was worse. Not only did he know that his famous premonitions always came true, but he also knew that he didn't know exactly what this one was about. For a clairvoyant, there's nothing worse than being in the dark. It's not natural. Derek knew that he was hardly being the life and soul of the party, but his guests had invited themselves, after all. He didn't really feel that he had to be responsible for their happiness. Which was just as well, really, for he was daily becoming more and more sure that no one was going to be happy ever again one day soon.

Meanwhile, Derek's guests had decided not, after all, to ask him what was wrong. Instead, they planned to hold a surprise party for him—guaranteed, they hoped, to cheer up the most miserable dinosaur. True, they were using Derek's food, Derek's flowers, Derek's balloons and Derek's exotic cocktails, but that hardly seemed relevant when a dinosaur was as rich as Derek.

The party was to be a surprise. The dinosaurs tried to look casual as they strolled around the pool as usual that afternoon. Hidden beneath the palm trees and ferns were all the party preparations. Smaller dinosaurs had to be restrained from investigating the nibbles.

At last, as the sun began to sink over Mount Mellifluous, Derek went indoors for a moment and his friends rushed to get everything ready. It looked brilliant. As Derek emerged from the house again, he was astonished to see crowds of dinosaurs, a full-size dinoswing band, and balloons everywhere.

"SURPRISE!" cried all his friends.

Derek smiled for the first time in weeks. And, as it turned out, the last time. Just then, the gloomy, doomy feeling he had been having for so long seemed to explode inside his head. The disaster was *here*. The disaster was *now*! At exactly the same moment, a small dinosaur looked up at the sky and pointed.

"I didn't know we were having fireworks, too! Oooh, isn't it pretty?"

A massive meteor *is* pretty. There's just one small problem about being on a planet in its path. Derek, seeing the end of the dinosaurs approaching, felt something very close to relief. Everything was clear now. He almost smiled again as he said, "Oh, so that's wha..."